Praise for Peter Handke and Across

"Peter Handke must be acknowledged as one of the major voices in contemporary fiction today."—*Partisan Review*

"If Ann Beattie has become America's premier observer of disaffected 1960s radicals, Handke has taken as his fictional territory a similar generation of discontented Europeans—individuals who can be characterized above all by their passivity, their intellectual frustration and their inability to take part in meaningful interaction with others."
—*San Francisco Chronicle*

"*Across* seems positively prophetic. Like Kafka, Camus and Sartre, Handke has set out to define contemporary man in terms of his dismay. *Across* accomplishes this in an acutely disturbing and effective way."—*People*

"Magical...an unusually involving book. It is a sheer pleasure to read and re-read, readily appreciable in the skillful translation by Ralph Mannheim."—*Choice*

"In power and vision and range, Peter Handke is the most important new writer on the international scene since Beckett."—Stanley Kaufmann, *Saturday Review*

"[Peter Handke] was and is, one of the most eminent narrative and dramatic writers of postwar Europe."
—*Boston Globe*

"Handke remains one of the most challenging and provocative writers in any language, and his status as such will only be enhanced by his latest novel, *Across*."—*Buffalo News*

About the Author

Peter Handke was born in Griffen, Austria, in 1942. After graduating from a Catholic seminary in 1959 he studied law at the University of Graz. Handke first attracted public notice in 1966 when he delivered an unprecedented attack on contemporary German writing at a seminar at Princeton University. That same year saw the publication of his first novel, *The Hornets*, and his first stage success, *Offending the Audience*. His other works include *Slow Homecoming* (1985), *The Weight of the World* (1984), *The Left Handed Woman* (1978), *A Moment of True Feeling* (1977), *Short Letter, Long Farewell* (1974), *A Sorrow Beyond Dreams* (1974), and *The Goalie's Anxiety at the Penalty Kick* (1972)—all of which are forthcoming from Collier Fiction. He is widely regarded as the most important postmodern writer since Beckett.

ACROSS

ACROSS

PETER HANDKE

Translated by Ralph Manheim

Collier Books
MACMILLAN PUBLISHING COMPANY
NEW YORK

Macmillan Publishing Company
866 Third Avenue, New York, N.Y. 10022
Collier Macmillan Canada, Inc.

Library of Congress Cataloging-in-Publication Data

Handke, Peter.
  Across.

  Translation of: Der Chinese des Schmerzes.
  I. Title.
PT2668.A5C4513   1987   833'.914   87-10960
ISBN 0-02-051540-5

Cover illustration © 1987 by David Montiel
Cover design by Lee Wade

First Collier Books Edition 1987

10 9 8 7 6 5 4 3 2

Printed in the United States of America

The Viewer Is Diverted

shut my eyes and out of the black letters the city lights took shape. Not the lights of the Old City, but the streetlamps that had just gone on in one of the many housing developments on the southern periphery. The development, consisting of two-story single-family houses, is situated on the big plain at the foot of the Untersberg. Long ago, this plain was a natural reservoir; then it silted up and became swampland—there are still swampy patches and ponds—and today it is known as the Leopoldskroner Moos. At first the streetlamps barely glimmer, then they flare up with a pure white light. By contrast, the arc lamps affixed to concrete poles at the eastern edge of the development, where a turnaround marks the end of the bus line, glow reddish-yellow. Between the bus terminus and the development lies a canal dating from the Middle Ages, fed by the Königsee and by one of the Untersberg brooks; this is the Alm Canal, the "noble Alm." The development lies right outside the city limits (just before the entrance, there's a sign with a diagonal line through the word "Salzburg"); it's called the Oak Tree Colony. All the streets take their names from trees: Alder Street, Willow Street, Birch Street, Fir Street. Only the road coming from the virtually uninhabited peat bog in the west has kept its old name: Cider Press Road. And within the development there are still a few of the old peat cutters' huts, some fallen into decay, some used for other purposes.

A trolleybus turns into the circle—a long, articulated vehicle. People get out, schoolchildren, locals, foreigners (who occupy the few wooden houses); all are in a hurry, only the children dawdle. They make their way in a cluster across the little canal bridge, followed by a few teenagers on their bicycles, which they left at the bus stop this morning. All together, they enter the Colony, which was almost deserted only a moment before and now suddenly seems inhabited. Dogs run barking to the garden gates. The phone booth at the edge of the Colony, which just now was dimly lit and empty, is darkened by phoners and people waiting to phone.

It's not dark yet. Throughout the city, the lights have as usual come on early. In the dip in the horizon between the Untersberg to the south and the Staufen to the west, there are orange-colored stripes. On the crest of the Untersberg, which is ordinarily dark at this hour, the cliffs glitter in triangular patches. Over the scree basin, below the peak, the last funicular is on its way down. The Staufen, farther away, beyond the German border, is blue-black; only the limestone furrows on its upper slopes are a lighter color; on the summit, the light of a mountain hut flickers. Actually there are two summits, the "big" and the "little" Staufen; as seen from the city, a few miles to the north, the distance between them is apparent. But here on the Moos one mountain is standing directly in front of the other, and the two together form a single pyramid that has no neighbor for a long way around. The summit of the Gaisberg stands similarly alone in the east. Except that, instead of being a pyramid, it's rounded, wooded, and topped with a plateau instead of a peak. On this side, the first star corresponds to the light in the hut on the Staufen. At the foot of the Gaisberg, just after the barren peat soil gives way to fertile

loam, the Salzach flows in the failing light. There on the
riverbank, not far from the boulder known as the Urstein,
I once met a man who, with a glance at the slightly overhanging cliff and the caverns in it, said: "The world is
old, isn't it, Herr Loser?"

With the light of that moment, silence fell. The warming emptiness that I need so badly spread. It was a
brightening, a primordial rising, so to speak. My forehead no longer needed a supporting hand. It wasn't exactly a warmth, but a radiance; it welled up rather than
spread; not an emptiness, but a being-empty; not so
much *my* being-empty as an empty form. And the empty
form meant: story. But it also meant that nothing happened. When the story began, my trail was lost. Blurred.
This emptiness was no mystery; but what made it effective remained a mystery. It was as tyrannical as it was
appeasing; and its peace meant: I must not speak. Under
its impulsion, everything (every object) moved into
place. "Emptiness!" The word was equivalent to the
invocation of the Muse at the beginning of an epic. It
provoked not a shudder but lightness and joy, and pre-
sented itself as a law: As it is now, so shall it be. In
terms of image, it was a shallow river crossing.

The emptiness became peopled with figures. On the
darkening street of the Colony, a young girl in baggy
blue trousers was walking straight into the last yellow
glow in the sky. An older woman on a bicycle turned in
from a side street, holding a full milk can in one hand
(there are a few isolated farms in the bog). An old man
was walking from his house to his garden gate and back,
changing his glasses on the way out and feeling his pulse

on the way back. As usual, the wind was from the west. It had come up strong in the late afternoon but now had dwindled to a soft breeze. Different varieties of trees grew one behind the other in the gardens; some of their branches swung from side to side, others up and down, so that in time one got an impression of uniform motion, perhaps of a loom or of saw blades. In one corner of my room a ball of dust lit by the floor lamp moved about, and in the sky a vapor trail drawn by a blinking metallic pencil flashed in the sun. At the bottom of the canal, clumps of moss drifted about. Out in the bog, a herd of deer jumped across a drainage ditch.

I live in two rooms in the development's only apartment house, situated just behind the canal bridge. The house was built in the decade after the war and is only three stories high; there's no elevator and no balcony. The ground floor is occupied by a supermarket. There's no other store in the vicinity. When I moved here, someone told me that, when asked for my address, the people at home said, "He's living at the last stop of the No. 5 line, upstairs from the SPAR." (This information, however, was not provided by my wife or children but by a neighbor woman.) My two rooms are indeed on the second floor, and sometimes at night I hear the vibration of the freezers downstairs. One of the rooms faces east, toward the canal and the bus stop, right behind which begins the level part of the Morzg forest, consisting mainly of dark spruce and underbrush; the other room has one window on the west and another on the north side; this last has a view of the city. From the Moos just then, all one could see of Salzburg was hidden by the so-called city mountains, the Festungsberg, the Mönchsberg, and the Rainberg; on their summits, one could see blinking ruby-colored warning lights. Though only a few miles distant, Salzburg seemed a long way off, because the thinly populated plain and the city mountains lay in between. The city mountains looked like mere hills, barely perceptible humps, and it was hard to imagine that they consist almost on every side of rather imposing cliffs, a fall from which means certain death. At the edge of the Old City, only a scattering of tourist buses were parked— there are long files of them during the day—and as the squares emptied of people, the gushing of the fountains became more audible. Not so long ago, all the city's fountains got their water from the Alm Canal, which at present drives one or two mills but is otherwise largely ornamental; there are plans to close it down entirely. The domes of the churches glittered copper-green in the evening light.

The fountains were turned on again only a few days ago. During the winter, they are covered with wooden scaffolding, and the most one can see through the cracks is the whitened eyes or nostrils of a stone horse. But now on the unpaved Residenzplatz one can again see all four horses with their outstretched or lowered heads, while here in the Colony the end of winter is marked by the depleted woodpiles outside the houses, which in the late fall had completely filled some of the vaulted doorways. In my little bedroom, facing east, there's a rack with a big shelf just for fruit; this, too, had been piled high at the onset of winter and was now pretty well thinned; the room no longer smelled of apples. The canal below had risen and the melting snow made the water even cloudier than usual. In a few days, summer time would go into effect. Yet the trees were still leafless. Only the elder-bushes were green, bluish at the tips. And another wintry feature: the sun still set to the left of the Staufen; as far as I was concerned, it wasn't summer until the sun had moved over to the right. The tip of the pyramid was a kind of dating stone or menhir. That day, it had snowed for a short while; higher up, the snow had stayed for several hours; there had been a distinct boundary, straight as a die, running all along the Untersberg, between the dark snowless woods below and the bright snowy woods above, with their clearly discernible tree-tops. Thick smoke was rising from nearly all the chimneys in the Colony, as if it were a country village. The different-colored smokes, blue, gray, and yellowish, merged in the air and drifted away like the trail of a locomotive. Words came to my mind—"Go home, people"—a variation on a poem two thousand years old, dealing, it is true, not with people but with cattle that had grazed their fill, and with the coming of the evening star.

I'm a teacher of ancient languages in Lehen, a quarter northwest of Salzburg, on the left bank of the Salzach. Lehen is the city's most densely populated district and is regarded as a working-class neighborhood. In the middle, there's a football field, the home ground of the team that used to be called Austria but now, like all Austrian football clubs, bears the name of the corporation that pays the players. As the crow flies, it's not very far to Lehen from the Oak Tree Colony here in the south. But the peat bog lies in between and there's no direct road across it, only the lengthwise Moos Road (the plan for a so-called southern tangent has been set aside for the time being). Consequently, since I haven't had a car for some time, I'm obliged, on my way to school, to take the bus into Salzburg and change to another bus. On the way home, though, I often walk through the Moos, cutting across the meadows at random until I come to the Alm Canal. From there, the towpath takes me straight to my house.

I haven't been teaching lately. Have I been dismissed or given a vacation or granted sick leave, or temporarily suspended? All I know is that there's no official term for my present status. Everything is up in the air, I say to myself. A few days ago, I knocked a man down in the street. One afternoon on Getreidegasse, which seemed less crowded than usual, I was overtaken by a man, who jostled me and immediately afterward turned to look in a shop window, with the result that we collided. To tell the truth, though, it wasn't a collision, because I could have stepped aside. I pushed the man intentionally, and it wasn't just a push, but more like a punch, a sudden impulse, so actually it's wrong to speak of intention. The man fell to the ground with a strange, almost inaudible cry of pain, then instantly stood up without my even offering him a helping hand. But while still on the ground he gave his assailant a quick look, as if he had understood. Then he vanished into a side street. Possibly he wasn't even a tourist, but a local. To an outsider, the scene must have looked like one of the usual collisions between pedestrians on this narrow street, only perhaps a little more violent.

In my decades as an adult, I have twice struck someone: once, on the night of a dance, I hit my girlfriend,
who had just kissed someone else before my eyes and in
public; and a few years before that—actually I was
an adolescent at the time—a boy from one of the lower
grades, whose study hall I had been appointed to super-
vise. It's true that as we left the dance the girl herself had
asked me to hit her, and my one blow, which came as a
surprise to me and which I did not repeat though she
asked me to, was in itself a solution. At the time, my act
gave me real satisfaction. Come to think of it, it wasn't an
act, but more like a reaction, occurring at the only possible moment, comparable to the jump or throw of an
athlete who for once knows with certainty: now or never.
So my conscience wasn't troubled and there was no question of reproach. Violent as my blow was, it inflicted no
pain—of that I'm sure—but only made both of us smart.
That was the turning point. We both recovered from our
paralysis. In that instance, I'm innocent. But the slap in
the study hall, brought on by some trifling provocation,
is still on my mind. Up until then, I had been a man like
other men; that slap showed me up as a criminal. The
look on the boy's face—though my blow hadn't really
struck home—has said to me down through the years:
Now I know you, now I know what kind of man you are,
and I won't forget it. It's not the look of a child or even
of a person; and it emanates not from two eyes but from
a single eye, which in all these years—though most of
the time unheeded—has never blinked. I saw that eye
again in the man I knocked down on Getreidegasse. It's
dark brown, not at all angry or hateful or avenging, just

inexorable; and its intention seemed to be to make me impossible, not to others but to myself. That eye, I sense, is right, and I sense that I, too, am right. The push I had given in the crowd didn't upset me for one moment. Afterward, as a matter of fact, I looked toward the vanishing point of the suddenly humped, meandering street, and saw my kindred climbing the deserted slope of the Gaisberg. My purpose here is, at last, to find myself confronting as a fact what for so long has pursued me as a mere phantasm. And "in suspense" doesn't mean "in danger," but precisely in suspense, or in a state of "in-decision," as it were.

The day after the incident on Getreidegasse, I obtained a temporary leave of absence from my job. The motive I gave was the urgent need to complete a paper that was to appear next spring in the *Salzburg Yearbook for Regional Studies.* This was an interim report on the excavation of a Roman villa in Loig, a village on the far side of the airfield. Though I'm not a trained archaeologist, I've spent a good part of my vacations working on digs all over the country, particularly the Hemmaberg in southern Carinthia, where I helped to remove the mosaic floor of the early Christian basilica. In the early days of my archaeological activity, an older archaeologist once said to me: "All you care about is *finding* something." It was in part this remark that impelled me to train myself at digs to look less for what was there than for what was missing, for what had vanished irretrievably—whether carried or merely rotted away—but was still present as a vacuum, as empty space or empty form. Thus, in the course of time, I acquired an eye for transitions that are ordinarily overlooked, even by professional archaeologists. Sometimes I playfully call myself a thresholdologist (or seeker after thresholds). This should not be taken only figuratively. I became in fact a student of house, church, and temple thresholds. I studied the thresholds of whole settlements, even though these last, as often when they are made of marble or granite, have been carried away, or, when they are made of wood, have rotted. In the field, I recognize the emplacements of former thresholds by hollows, color gaps, and traces of wood. My work is not merely incidental; once thresholds are located, the whole ground plan can be deduced; they provide boundaries that indicate the original layout of a building or a whole village.

A glass on my desk contains some sawdust, the remains of a threshold I discovered on the Hemmaberg and wrote my first paper about. Discovering and describing thresholds became a passion with me. During the school year I often devoted an afternoon to it, helping on digs in the immediate vicinity, such as the Celtic Dürrnberg near Hallein or, only recently, the "Roman Road" in Loig. I was usually rather tired the next day, but that actually benefited my teaching; it made me calm and alert, and I listened to my pupils, just as they listened to me.

My report on the Loig dig was just about finished, including the photographs and the drawings of cross sections and horizontal sections with the small initials A.L. (Andreas Loser) in the lower right-hand corner. The task assigned to me was making measurements of the vestibule; describing and interpreting the floor mosaics was the work of the professionals. "Access to the villa was provided by a door so-and-so many Roman feet wide, with a masonry base for the formerly present wooden threshold. A space so-and-so many Roman feet wide and so-and-so many Roman feet high was set aside for it at the foot of the east wall." Time and again, while I was doing this work, the black knotholes in the floor-boards of my room looked to me like colored mosaic stones, and once a fresco appeared in the white wall: Iphigenia, holding a statue of the goddess Artemis, on her way to the sea, before escaping to Greece with her brother—a mural from Pompeii, intimating to me that my measurements had not been entirely useless. When toward the end I looked up from my paper for a moment, the Untersberg with its sunlit crest was situated in the ancient world, and I saw the corresponding alluvial cones at the foot of the Staufen.

My desk had been cleared. It's a small, light-colored office model with a chipboard top and steel legs, and it blended nicely with its surroundings. Beside the glass with the sawdust in it, there is an elongated piece of wood with holes at one end, rounded edges, and slanting grooves of varying width—a so-called hand fondler, carved years ago by my son (more or less as a school exercise), blackened from handling, but still smelling of fresh wood, just as the brown, fist-sized, hardened lump of clay beside it, whenever I pick it up, takes on the smell of the damp gully from which it was taken years ago. Written in pencil on the clay is the Greek word "Galene," meaning "the calm, radiant sea," which, according to the philosopher Epicurus, can be taken as a model of existence (the man sitting over it interpreted the luminous graphite word more as a kind of call to order). The last in this row of objects is an egg-shaped lump of clay which not so long ago was broken from a dried thornbush on a Mediterranean island: a puzzling object, a mixture of sand and tiny stones that some sort of insect may have built around a branch of the thornbush, which now on my desk is still inside it, forming an arrow, whose tip emerges at the other end of the egg. A number of deep holes give it the appearance of an ocarina, except that the holes have no outlet. They seem, deep inside, to be joined in a single hollow, though the passages are so crooked that the eye cannot follow them. The interior of these passages glows an intense bright red that seems to enamel their walls. Once, when someone blew into one of the holes, the long feelers of an unknown, black-armored insect darted out of a neighboring hole, and immediately retracted. All these objects might be termed my "callers to order," because, by pleasantly diverting me now and again, they save me from losing myself entirely in my work.

The lump of clay with the round black hiding places lay there like an abandoned primeval necropolis where nothing remains but lizards. The lamp illumined the desk, which was bare except for the four objects. The rest of the room, ordinarily unlit, lay in half darkness. In the neighboring apartments, next door and upstairs, water faucets sounded one after another. On the west and east edge of the plain, where the two railroad lines recede into the distance, a long-drawn-out whistling coupled with a rumbling could be heard at regular in-

tervals; and on the express highway skirting the Untersberg, a roaring and a blowing of horns. Some of the
apartment-house windows were open to the balmy evening air; a fat man in a white undershirt was leaning out
of one of them, smoking; in another stood a clay jar,
holding a papyrus plant that shot up like fireworks, its
star-shaped greenery strikingly vivid against the yellow
sky; in the window downstairs a caged parrot, luminous
blue in the twilight, sat silently shaking its head; one of
the open windows was empty.

Why did I leave my family? Was I sent away? Was
it my idea to desert the three of them? Was there any
reason for the separation (which has never become an
official divorce)? Did I leave for good, or only for the
time being? Haven't I got the daily routine of each one of
them in my head, as though I were secretly still living
with them? Whenever I run into my son or daughter in
the street, isn't their first question, put without emphasis,
rather as a matter of course: "When are you coming
over?"—the kind of thing one doesn't say to just anyone. Would I live with them again someday? To all those
questions I have had no answer, though I believe I know
one thing: a final separation will never be possible. In any
case, my name, "Loser" (common all over Austria, and
also frequent in the phone books of northern Italy,
especially in such cities as Gorizia and Trieste), does
not in my opinion suggest someone who gets rid (*los*)
of something, and certainly not a loser (in the English
sense); it is, I believe, connected with the dialect verb
losen, meaning "listen" or "hark." In the Salzkammergut
there's a mountain called Loser, which starts as a gently

rounded hill but culminates in a massive rocky dome; a seemingly unscalable fortress, with sides so steep that they remain almost free of snow in the winter, the few snowy patches suggesting false windows.

On the other hand, I have no idea what my wife is up to, what people she sees, what kind of work she's doing. Unlike me, she takes easily to new languages—has she become a translator? Is she going on with her studies, which were interrupted by our marriage? Is she guiding tourists around the town? (I once thought I saw her, holding an umbrella over her head and leading a group.) Is she lecturing at the People's University? I never ask. Even before, I seldom asked her a question. That may be what led to our separation. Inability to ask questions is often my problem. And yet I'm made up almost entirely of questions. But, as a rule, I regard every question as the wrong one and I can't get it out of my mouth. Or then again, something in me rebels against the kind of questioning that might better be called pumping.

Yet I keep going back to the house where my family live. Though considerable time may have elapsed, there's no great excitement when I come in; only the conventional evening greetings of people who have been going their separate ways during the day. Once, when I'd been away for six months, my son in his room just looked up briefly from something or other and said: "Well?"

The house is the kind of place where an old-time teacher might have lived—it's painted yellow, with pointed gables and a wooden veranda that serves as a winter garden. It's in Gois, which lies a few fields and pastures to the west of Loig with its Roman villa. The

guidebooks list Gois as a suburb of Salzburg, but it's a
good hour's walk from the center of the city and gives
the impression of a remote peasant village. The only
connection with the Old City is by bus, and the last bus
leaves the city before the end of the working day. The
road is narrow and little traveled; for a short stretch
before the village, it degenerates into a dirt path through
the fields. What one sees first of the village is a scattering of farmhouses; there are few new buildings. The
walls of the farmhouses are of porous, untrimmed stone
in various shades of gray, inlaid with small black slag
stones. The doors are made of a kind of pudding stone,
and the thresholds of a reddish marble with light-colored
veins and numerous ammonite inclusions. This gives the
farms an old-fashioned look, as though they belonged
to a different period from the one-family houses in their
midst, as though they had been built before the Gothic
church on the knoll. They form a kind of unit with the
knoll in the flat country, a strange formation suggesting
a prehistoric mound. Round about there are fields, their
base lines pointing toward Salzburg. Of the city one can
see only the castle, which from there looks like a bright,
delicately shaped stone crown. The fields, on which more
vegetables are grown than grain, seem to extend almost
to the city limits, thus giving the impression of a vast
plantation, capable of supplying the whole city. At dusk,
the red lights in the belfry go on—warning signals for
planes. On its way back to town, the last bus from
Grossgmain, dark inside, stops in front of the village
inn, whose curtains, as customary throughout Austria,
are drawn immediately after sunset. Despite the short

row of streetlamps, no village for miles around is quieter in the evening. Since the church is not a parish church, there are no evening bells. On the other hand, the stars over the fields are brighter here than anywhere else. The constellations can be distinguished at a glance; one doesn't have to look for them. And the soft rustling of the bushes by the roadside is clearly audible. Seen from the city, Gois consists only of the red lights on the belfry, barely distinguishable from the harsh yellow row of lamps beyond it, marking the Walserberg Autobahn overpass.

What stops me from going back to the school when my paper is finished? Don't I need my daily work, or at least my presence there, the comfort of habitual turns of phrase? Hasn't my place always been in an interlocking collective, each member of which, however, keeps his distance from the others? Doesn't the public sphere, without which I am incomplete, begin at the school door? Isn't my ride to my public existence the natural thing for me, and doesn't it open up the possibility of a satisfactory way back? In any event, I don't regard myself as a loner, it doesn't suit me to be a free-lancer, and certainly not an independent scholar (though, early in my studies, someone advised me to become one). I know I should work with others, not just occasionally, but day after day. Only among others does something resembling a world appear to me, if only in the briefly flaring brown of a lichen in the Antarctic. One day perhaps a stranger from the plains, on his way to a still-undiscovered city, will approach our local castle (that forbidding hulk), and the canal at his feet will flow through timeless lowlands, or through the Chinese limestone province of Kwei-lin. Did I, for that, need a kind, *my* kind, of job? But now will I have another few days to myself? Won't it soon be Easter vacation, in any case?

I opened both my workroom windows and let the sounds in. From the north, not far away, came the ringing of the bells at Gneis, which is already within the city limits; from the west, almost as audible because of the wind, the bells of the Moos church, which was much farther away. The manager of the store downstairs was moving boxes and chalked signs back inside. A train in the distance didn't whistle, but gave out a sound as of someone blowing into his cupped hands—a brewery locomotive on the way back to its shed for the night. High over the foothills of the Bavarian Alps, the plane from Zurich came into view with a violent blinking of lights; the runway was brightly lit to receive it; the plane went into a slow glide and its landing lights flared up; a few seconds after it put down, the din filled the whole plain.

Now I had time. Facts and questions crystallized. This having-time wasn't a feeling; it was a resolution: the resolution of all my contradictory feelings. It was a jolt and a widening; disengagement and devotion; defenselessness and the ability to resist; quiescence and enterprise. Its occurrence was rare. Perhaps what is commonly called a "state of grace" should be called a "state of having time." It had its counterpart in a traditional paraphrase of the threshold concept as a "transi-

tion between privation and riches." In a state of having-
time, a murmur spread over the countryside, colors
shone, grasses trembled, moss cushions puffed up.

Holding my plate on my lap, I ate in the kitchen,
which was too small for a table. A colony of daddy longlegs adhered to the walls, clinging to the grainy limestone with their spindly legs, which suggested clock
hands. Unceasingly, they swung to and fro, giving the
whole kitchen the air of a clockmaker's workshop, filled
with pendulums and silent ticking. From time to time
the clocks shifted their position, or else one would stand
long-legged over another, the two of them swinging together. Down on the tile floor, several of the evidently
short-lived creatures lay on their backs, radial forms
no longer—some with legs folded in dying, but quiver-
ing violently; others, already dead, had twined their
legs tightly around their already dried-out bodies:
mummylike balls, visibly gathering dust. The gaps left
by the fallen were immediately taken by others, evidently newborn, brighter in color than the rest and con-
spicuously smaller, which joined at once in the general
ticking. These creatures are known to me from excavation sites, where they often keep those working in the
galleries company with their pendular motion. Here in
my place they serve as household pets, as does the un-
identified insect inside the ball of sand on my desk; by
making me look up and pause in my work, they, like
sundials, help me to "have time." If it was possible in
the past to worship (or at least to see) the sun in beetles,
why not in these harmless spiders that spin no webs?

These are animals which, even when they appear in large numbers, provoke no fear, but only surprise and amusement. "Daddy longlegs, patron of threshold seekers," I said in the night-dark kitchen to the hum of the fluorescent lamp, to the ticking of the real clock (on the electric stove), to the clicking of the trolleys on a bus that was just pulling out from the turnaround down below.

And then the ticking and swinging of the daddy longlegs tied in with the poem, from which, as usual at the end of the day, I slowly, word by word, read a few lines —Virgil's poetic treatise on agriculture, known as *The Georgics* (I hope to translate it when I'm old and retired from other work): the lines from *The Georgics* turn time back for me, or give it a different meaning.

The express purpose of the work, as stated at the beginning, is instruction: about the dates for plowing, binding the vines, and so on, about cattle raising and agriculture; at the same time, it is conceived as a poem. This poem can indeed teach us a great deal about the laws of nature, and its teaching cannot grow old. For instance, a vine outside our house in Gois was languishing until in *The Georgics* I came across a line I had disregarded up until then, to the effect that "grain" demands "firm soil," whereas the vine requires "loose soil." And our worry about the bay tree in the garden whose leaves fell at the slightest midsummer breeze was dispelled by Virgil's casual remark about the pomegranate tree, which according to him resembles the bay, except that it smells different and that "no wind can tear off its reeling leaves" (suggesting that such loss of leaves was characteristic of the bay tree and not a symptom of disease).

However, it is not from these agricultural precepts that I derive the lesson I really care about, but from the poet's enthusiasm (never uncontrolled) for the things that still matter: the sun, the earth, rivers, woods, trees and shrubs, domestic animals, fruits (along with jars and baskets), utensils and tools. In these objects, justice, before vanishing from the world, left its trace; thus, far from the weapons that divide man from man (the usual word for "weapon" stands here for peaceable implements), every single thing in the poem, removed once and for all from history, distanced from other things and at the same time held in free association with them, gives me access to a very different story—usually invoked with an epithet: the slow-growing olive tree, the smooth linden, the bright-colored maple, the loose marl, the savage east wind, the air-clearing north wind, the dew-giving moon. Similarly, a box hedge, trimmed round or square in accordance with present-day tastes, conceals (or preserves) within itself the "swaying box tree," which I am able to reconstruct on the basis of the epithet that does justice to the thing. Virgil, it is said, created his verses in the manner of a she-bear bringing forth her cubs, by hard labor during birth and even greater labor in "licking them clean," so as to give his progeny its existential form. And since poetry should above all be congruent with things, these verses never cease to revive for me, the reader, the existence of the things they sing of. Goats with their heavy udders—are they not "struggling across the threshold" at this very moment? Are not cows once again "obliterating their tracks with their tails as they make their way" over some country road? As I looked up, a car from somewhere turned onto the canal bridge and, thanks to Virgil's verses, gleamed a special blue.

The circle of lamplight on my desk; the bicycle stand down at the bus stop (replacing the pyramid of the Staufen, which had vanished in the darkness); the driver sitting in the waiting bus; the dog lying in the garden of the house next door; the stacks of shopping bags in the supermarket; the birds roosting in the bushes; the dangling creepers on the Salzach meadows; the emptiness of the long wooden bench in front of a farmhouse; the crisscrossing paths on the plain; the crookedness of the quarter moon (in place of the blinking airplane that was there before); the green spirals in the vegetable gardens; the sinkholes in the Untersberg karst (an inverted pyramid); the slow rotation of the disk in the electric meter; the falling dew; the gravel banks deposited on alluvial cones; the body lying in state; the winged ram.

Leaving the book open and the lamp lit, I went downstairs. I sat with the driver in the stationary bus. Outside, on the bench in the shelter, lay a folded newspaper; under it, a seemingly congealed puddle of vomit. When one looked at it a while, the face of the almost naked young woman on the billboard beside it became open and expectant. On the railing of the canal bridge, a couple were sitting pressed close. The man had his arm around the woman. She was wearing white patent-leather shoes which, as they kissed, protruded motionless from above the bottom crossbar.

Now and then, the hazel catkins at the edge of the woods gave off a yellowish dust, without being visibly stirred by the wind. Many of the darker, barely nascent catkins on the lone birch were shaped like bird's claws. The moon was tinged with red, which according to *The Georgics* meant storms (a whitish coloration would have foreshadowed rain).

By then, the buses were running only at infrequent intervals. This one had stopped for so long at the terminus that it seemed to be waiting for someone. Then a young girl with a red coat and far-echoing high heels emerged from the Colony and got in; her eyes were ringed with black and she had pink circles of powder on her cheeks. During the ride she stood beside the driver, occasionally resting her hand on his shoulder and grazing him with her hip. The ground fog drifted across the road, as often happens in the evening on the plain, with periods during which one could see quite clearly. After a few stops, I got off near the illuminated glass wall of the indoor tennis courts in Gneis, still far from the Old City. The girl behind me said: "An Indian"—which was startling, because, only a short while before, a child coming toward me in the street had shouted out the same word to its mother: "Look, an Indian!"

Behind the high, illuminated wall of the tennis-court building lies the municipal cemetery, in the darkness an elongated mass of bare trees that could be mistaken for a park; the lighted candles on the graves were invisible. The tennis courts resounded with thumped balls, shouts, and running steps. Now and then, the white shape of a shoulder or a hip could be seen on the opaque glass. The air ducts of the snack bar adjoining the sports stadium gave forth a roar of voices, suggesting an over-crowded beer hall rather than so small a room. The serried cars in the parking lot were wet with dew. The wide open field on the city side of the cemetery kept disgorging strollers and joggers, who either headed for nearby cafés or vanished into one of the new apartment houses, the biggest of which were not even as tall as the poplars (there is still not a single high-rise building in the entire Moos district). When the bus drove on, the overhead wires showered sparks at the crossings, and when it was gone, the wires far down the road continued to flash in the headlights of passing cars—a trail of light in the night sky, enlivened by the spiraling light-colored pigeons in the mist around the tennis-court build-ing and the moonlit clouds between the steeples of the Gneis church. The evenings are lively in this suburban section, quite unlike those of the Old City, where the streets and squares are almost deserted at this hour and the few remaining passersby are excessively quiet when they are not shouting. There was a smell of wood fires (or was it a last remnant of the smoke from the crema-torium, which during the day could often be seen rising above the treetops?). Buzzing monotonously, a single-engine airplane described an arc over the inhabited zone (this time there would be no crash; not here, at least).

To one side, tennis courts and cemetery; to the other, the Alm Canal. At the foot of its embankment, there's a building that looks like a home, the Canal Tavern. To reach it, one passes through a vacant, treeless field, across which the tavern's luminous sign can be seen from far off, at dusk soft-white against the eastern sky, in the darkness glaring—an outlandish signal on the low house at the edge of the field. The café is run by a pensioner, but he has put it in his wife's name (for fear of losing his pension). The front garden is even smaller than those in the nearby development, and the jukebox is not in the café proper but in the entrance, which has the size and proportions of a vestibule in a private house. Beside the jukebox, there is a similarly lighted vitrine with food in it.

As I had walked part of the way through the fields, I kicked the caked mud off my shoes before going in. Here, too, the indoor sounds—abrupt bursts of unanimous laughter, competing shouts, the gurgling espresso machine, and in brief pauses the suddenly tenacious keynote of the jukebox—gave the impression of a tightly packed crowd. But when I went in, I found the two low-ceilinged rooms almost empty. At one table sat four card players, all wearing hats, and at the next, three young women, one well advanced in pregnancy, one with a faint mustache and hair dyed reddish-brown, the third with a dachshund at her feet. A fifth man, keeping the card players company, was holding an accordion, on which he softly accompanied the card game, using different chords for different phases of play. The landlord was leaning against the bar; a pencil attached by a string to his belt dangled down below his knees. Piles of illustrated magazines on the window ledges reached to the tops of the potted plants. There were no newspapers in racks as in the cafés of the Old City; if anyone asked for a paper, the landlord brought his own copy from his apartment on the upper floor. Both rooms front on the canal embankment, which extends well above the lower edge of the windows and keeps out most of the daylight. The few tables are oversized, as in a country tavern, an encouragement to "sit down and join us," and the table-cloths have a pattern usual in taverns, a white lozenge against a larger, darker one; on the tablecloths lie piles of beer coasters and a wicker basket containing condi-ments and wooden toothpicks (though no longer made of "pliable barberry wood"). The light in the rooms was dim, in striking contrast to the garish sign outside; only at the table, under that lamp over there, was it somewhat brighter.

After a day of working alone, it does me good to go to some café, if only because of the place names that are dropped here and there in the table conversation: Mauterndorf, Abtenau, Gerlin, Iben. Then, in my weari-ness, I manage to show that glimmer of interest in everything around me that makes me, or so I believe, inconspicuous; no one, I feel sure, will turn to me, let alone against me. When I leave, no one will talk about me. But my presence will have been noticed.

I sat in my usual corner, with a view of the two small groups, and also, through the cleft in the curtains, out into the open. There in the northern sky gleamed the gray prison wall of the castle, toward which the canal flows in gentle meanders, in the foreground traversed by one of its many bridges. Two cars were standing side by side on the hump of the bridge, the drivers talking to each other through open windows, as if they had just met. Between them slithered a moped, whose rider's body while on the bridge seemed airier for a moment. Then the bridge was empty. An old man and an old woman sat on a bench on the embankment, which oddly enough, like all the benches along the canal, faced away from the water. After a while one of the small, box-shaped electric buses, whose routes mark the boundaries of the city proper, appeared on the bridge with a single passenger, who seemed to be sitting on the floor. A moment later, the blue light of an ambulance blinked at the same spot so intensely that it was reflected on the teeth of a laughing woman inside the café.

Here, too, there are houses occupied by people from southern countries. A black-eyed, brown-skinned adolescent came in with a child who looked like him, and went to the bar, where he exchanged a large empty wine bottle for a full one. He introduced the child as his uncle and talked about himself. He went to the local public school; the special class that had been organized for foreigners was known as the "color class," not because of the crayons, which are virtually the only teaching aids in use, but because of the different skin colorations represented. The principal, said the boy, is proud of this class; he had even arranged for it to have a special entrance, and the hours are different from those of the Austrian classes. So many drawings had accumulated by the end of the year that not only the walls but all the cabinets were full of them. The drawings exhibited in the auditorium showed not only foreignness but also the beauties of the host country, which the natives had often lost their eye for. The school with the color class was in Schallmoos at the other end of town, behind the Kapuzinerberg, and foreign children were sent there from all over the city; one of the pupils had been run over and killed yesterday; it was in today's paper. Most of the drawings were about war: Turks against Greeks, Iranians against Iraqis; Yugoslavs against Albanians. While the boy was talking, the child with him picked up a log and fired bursts in all directions.

On their way out, the two of them stopped in the corridor and inserted a coin in the jukebox, which had one record of Macedonian folk music: the café was filled with a melody without beginning or end. And something that had never happened before: the café turned into the garden terrace of a restaurant on the west bank of the Jordan. The terrace was empty except for crackling gusts of sand, the slapping of palm leaves, and the sound of music without beginning or end. Eastward lay the Dead Sea depression; the pregnant woman straightened up in her chair, gathered her long hair together and piled it on top of her head; while the record was playing, she was a woman on the shores of the Dead Sea, an embodiment of the sea itself.

The outer door opened and closed. The adolescent appeared in the cleft between the curtains. Outside, on the embankment, he was holding the wine bottle in one hand and, without wavering, was carrying his uncle piggyback. Resting his log on his carrier's shoulder, the child aimed into the darkness.

The card players had stopped playing, but remained

seated in the same order. They began to talk quietly among themselves, without shouting or laughing; almost voicelessly. The landlord took the last orders and joined them. One of the players, as I hadn't noticed before, was a woman. The youngest of the men moved closer to her. The three women at the next table had already gone. The little dog had lain down against the table leg and was sleeping. The ventilator on the canal side was whirring. An Asian in an orange plastic cape came in with a bundle of newspapers fresh off the press; a moment later, he had vanished; no one was in a reading mood just then.

Then came a slowdown, which seemed to suit those present; one by one, all made ready to leave, and then suddenly, after a moment of hesitation, they were in no hurry at all. It was an interval of patience, during which even the landlord stopped looking at the clock. The woman, who, apparently out of sorts, had just thrown the cards down in front of the man, began to toy with his shirt collar, and he kissed each one of her knuckles; the others at the table spoke to one another softly and, at most, looked at the couple from time to time, not out of the corners of their eyes but wide-eyed, almost dreamily. The landlord's wife, who had finished cleaning up, stood in the white light of the open kitchen door; she was wearing high rubber boots. One of the men at the table inspected the palm of his hand, the lines of which were black with soot or oil. Another let out something resembling a yodel; not of joy or sorrow, but of weariness; the weariest of all yodels.

Then all had gone home except the lovers. In the

kitchen, the landlord discussed the shopping for the next day with his wife. In the toilet, a late guest was standing at the washbasin; seen from behind, the chamois beard on his hat wavered, though the man was hardly moving.

Meanwhile, man and woman sat face to face, with a seriousness that gave them Egyptian profiles. The cautious though steady tightening of their enfolding arms suggested slowly closing tendrils. The man touched the woman's neck with his fingertips, as though trying to feel her heartbeat there. From under motionless eyelids, she stared into his eyes, while at the same time, in a quick exchange, one spoke softly and urgently to the other. After that, they sat motionless, face to face, no longer recognizable, for an eternity, like the sun and moon in old engravings. Just for this man, this woman must have been the most beautiful woman in the world! For another eternity, red colored both their cheeks until —in simultaneous movement—he bent over her and she leaned not only her head but her whole body to one side, like a woman getting ready, in self-abandon, to rip the bearskin off the wall to cover herself and her lover with. "And the greatest of all things happened"—a paraphrase for bodily union occurring in shepherds' tales. But did those two at the table in the Canal Tavern need to be bodily united? Weren't they already one flesh? A small yellow pencil sped almost inaudibly downward, like a bird's beak.

Afterward I lingered for a while outside on the embankment road, my back to the tavern with the drawn curtains. The couple's voices were in the whirring of the ventilator: not a whispering or a murmuring, not really voices, just sounds, now higher, now lower, unintelligible yet penetrating; punctuated distinctly by the landlord's voice: "Table 10."

The patch of meadow on the other side of the canal was white with fog in spots, while the rest of it was quite open. The fog didn't lift, but lay impenetrably dense on the ground, barely cloaking the tips of the grass. Two triangular ears were all that showed of a cat that was lurking there. However, a movement was discernible in the mist, not a steady flow of swaths, but a to-and-fro, a reaching out and a pulling back, a sudden surging up and flattening out, as though the fog were not fog at all but smoke from the peat smoldering under the grass. Sometimes the creeping whiteness seemed to boil up above eye level, as though from the subterranean bubbling of a geyser. Above it, the night was clear; the houses at the far end of the meadow rose out of their steamy foundations with contours all the sharper, and seemed more houselike than usual; and in my mind there was no longer a national boundary between me and the pyramid of the Staufen, now pointed in the moonlight.

The fog accompanied me on my way home. The way leads upstream, always along the canal; just once, it crosses a bridge to the other bank, and then crosses back again by the next bridge. At first, there's a tarred road on the embankment, then a street belonging to the Colony, and finally, as far as the turnaround, a path for pedestrians and bicycles. Strangely enough, the fog never crossed the canal; the layers to the left and the right didn't mingle, the water formed a sort of fog shed (each patch of meadow, pasture, or bog generated its own fog, differing from others in color and shape); on the watercourse itself, there were only transparent clouds of vapor. Suddenly a patch of woods, which only a moment before had been an island in the pond of mist, stood free in the black country, as though the underbrush had swallowed the whiteness. The fog piled up behind a fence as though stopped by an obstacle or a threshold. In an orchard, its meandering flow connected a tumbledown bakehouse with a beehive, whose wooden squares, despite the dark night all around, gleamed in every color above the milky whiteness. Once, when I stood still and looked down, the fog was knee-high and I couldn't see my own feet; yet at the same time I clearly saw the pattern of the kitchen wall tiles in the lighted windows of a house nearby: roses. With all the many continuing sounds, bicycle dynamos, television sets, home carpentry, the silence was so great that a cow with its long-drawn-out mooing seemed to be blowing into a picture-book horn; pictures of an autumn fire, a rainstorm, another watercourse. The horn ended in my own breast; the usual breastplate wasn't there anymore.

At regular intervals, the canal was bordered by small wooden signboards covered with posters of the various local political parties (one more election was in the offing); for the most part, portraits of local politicians with slogans you pick up in spite of yourself and can't get out of your head. Mechanically, I kicked one of the signboards. It proved to be unanchored and my little kick almost knocked it over. Without looking around, I picked it up and threw it into the canal, where it sank instantly. The next one had tapering legs and was planted more firmly in the ground. Nevertheless, I was sure—as sometimes when opening a can—that I could get it out with one tug and tip it into the canal (as indeed I did). I disposed of all the other signboards in the same way. In the autumn, when the Alm would go dry for a month, the legs would rise up out of the muck, the discolored scraps of paper would swell, and the dredger that cleans the canal would pile all this junk, along with the usual tires, old clothes, and dead fish, onto garbage trucks. I once asked someone who knows me well whether he thought me capable of committing murder, and now the answer came back to me: "Committing, no. Wanting to, yes." Was this a case of wanting to commit murder? No. Was it mere caprice, or, as they say, "malicious mischief"? No. In any event, while walking, I kept saying aloud a word which, I was well aware, did not provide the right answer either: "revenge"; with the addition: "I have a right to look at the water. By obstructing my view of the water, you are infringing on my rights." (My inner cry at first sight of the face—silent, to be sure—on the poster: "Shut up!")

Since then, I've only once done anything comparable; that was in connection with a slogan on a church wall (though all I did then was to take out my pencil in passing and cross it out). Now, with my penknife, I removed the red-and-white trail markers—*European Cross-Country Trail, Bohemian Forest—Stone Sea—Carnic Alps*—from the willows on the riverbank and threw them after the wooden stands. I did the same with a birdhouse, a theater showcase, a poster advertising a recently opened hairdressing establishment, showing models that might have been portraits of wanted terrorists. Finally, with my lighter, I set fire to the gable-shape sign planted in the ground outside a house under construction, announcing that a corporation was interested in "land suitable for development" (phosphorescent letters in the darkness), and looked on as it smoldered and then really burned, along with its gable. No one was watching me, and if they had been, they might have thought they were witnessing some anonymous official act.

Never have the trunks of willow trees looked so thick to me as after that. The little wooden frames projecting over the canal, formerly emplacements for clothes washing, looked a little like docks. What had become of the boat that went with them? The wood-sheathed bed of the Alm was itself the ship, sailing past and standing still at the same time. The water didn't flow, but stirred far and wide. The bark of the willows buckled like that of cork oaks ready to be harvested and made into life jackets. Willows go with rivers . . . willows rich in withes . . . from the withes are fashioned docks for bees . . . so the bees, "when blown into the water by the east wind, can climb out and spread their wings in the summer sun . . ."

Effective facts, or magic formulas that have lost their efficacy? A form of existence with the force of law, or nothing more than pretentious incantations? The ants which, betokening imminent showers, "carry their eggs from the anthills to safety over a narrow path"; the girls who, while spinning at night, "foresee the coming storm by the sputtering of oil in their lamp and the moldy fungus that forms around the wick"—images acting forever anew, or old ones that have lost their force? Striking, in any case, how the repetitions in current phrases usually impress me as something evil, pathological, or even criminal. Could one not, on the other hand, speak of refreshing repetition as opposed to wearisome repetition; voluntary repetition as opposed to forced repetition? The possibility of repetition as opposed to the danger of repetition? Shine for me, hard hazelbush. Glide hither, lithe linden tree. Rounded elderbush, prosper under the protection of the willows. Here is my other word for repetition: "rediscovery."

Back home, I ate an apple in the dark; drank a glass of water; watered the plants. The bicycle stand at the bus terminus was empty now. The last bus had left for the city without passengers. The wires would crackle no more, though for a long time they swung to and fro. The moon went down—time to watch the stars. I used to attend the meetings of the Salzburg Friends of the Stars regularly. They were usually held at the top of Morzg Hill, which then was the darkest spot in the vicinity, ideal for observing the night sky. Later, as the glow of the city lights affected a larger and larger area, we moved to the more distant Gaisberg. But after a while there was no proper darkness even there; a diffuse glow veiled the starry firmament, and in the end the Friends of the Stars broke up. Nevertheless, the episode was useful to me; soon after I joined, the group leader gave me a good lesson with regard to my way of searching the sky: "You're always in such a hurry to identify, instead

of just gazing for a while." On the other hand, I have
to admit that, after observing the stars for any length of
time, I'm relieved to get back to the murmuring of the
trees down below.

Now that the moon was down, there seemed to be
gaps in the sky: deep-black empty spaces. The great
winter constellations had not yet risen. The plain down
below, except for the chain of lights on the Moos highway, was almost dark; the airfield no longer glittered;
the warning lights on the "city mountains" had been
switched off; not even a charter plane would land now.
Only the border crossing on the Autobahn would shine
glaring yellow all night, and with it the not far distant,
pale-white gate of the Walserfeld army post, which at
first sight looked like another border crossing; when a
car didn't happen to be crossing the border, the deserted
concrete road, lit from far above, could be mistaken for
the army post's execution ground. The villages of the
plain had vanished in the darkness, but their supposedly
Celtic names—Anif, Grödig, Morzg, Gneis, Loig, Wals,
Gois—would take on life again. My son once said that
those place names made him think of the names of trees.

Sounds were still heard, but all, even the short,
dreamy piping of the titmice outside the window, kept
their distance from one another. None had the character
of a bang, a crash, a clatter, or a screech; and they
sounded regularly, whether far away or in the immediate vicinity, as though reporting for duty; first the
motorcycle on the Autobahn, then the refrigerator case
in the supermarket; then the farm dog; and still another,
high above the plain, was the distant thudding of a

boulder blasted off the Untersberg by the overnight freeze and rolling down into the cirque. Each of these sounds fell into the total silence, which it further enhanced; and from the black night, in slow sequences punctuated by long intervals of silence, emerged something akin to Far Eastern calligraphy, undifferentiated black, but formally rigorous and luminous, brightening behind the lids of the man listening as he fell asleep.

But deep in the night—all sound spent, the writing long since gone—after he had suddenly started up and rushed to the window, came the pervasive suffering which canceled out everything that had gone before, and which with its endlessness exceeded even the gurgling death cry. And a cry there really was; a cry, a screaming, a shrieking. Someone is crying out. No, not someone: a child. The endless cries of a child out there, somewhere on the plain. They do not come from the immediate vicinity, but undoubtedly someone in the Colony (and far beyond, in other neighborhoods) is being wakened by them from deepest sleep, in spite of doubly closed windows and barred shutters. And now we all hear the child's cries and hold our breath (even though in the morning we act as if nothing had happened). It's no ordinary crying or mewling, nor is it a wordless screaming; it seems more like a call, a repeatedly bellowed two-syllable word, by which someone is being called. The child is helpless. It can do nothing but cry out that one name. It seems to be out of doors or at least in a wide-open house, unable to stir from the spot. This spot can be pinpointed. Recollecting the existence in the region of a home for so-called handicapped children comforts me only briefly. No help is possible; one can only be a witness. And the cries persist. They become so pervasive that the hundred (and more) caverns in the mass of the Untersberg—the ice caves, the tunnels, the chimneys, the clefts, the windholes—burst into a single cry hole, extending from cave to cave. Here in my room, the elusive red-scissored insect slips into the recesses of the sand ball, and in the intervals between cries a fat fly seems to thud over and over again against the windowpanes. Now the child is screaming the extreme suffering which in adults takes the form of innermost muteness; if every sufferer screamed like that, the world would have gone into a tailspin long ago. And in the natural way of things, this child will somehow have to stop crying eventually. (It has indeed stopped.) In the restored silence, the starry firmament will? will not? be restored to its proper shape. The next noise, in any case, still in total darkness, will be the reliable clatter and bumping of the garbage trucks. But I'll have been a witness nonetheless: I'll have seen how, for the duration of those cries, Birch Street, Fir Street, Willow Street, all the streets of the Colony, had only a single name—Nameless Street.

The Viewer Takes Action

The monthly tarok game was scheduled for the Wednesday of Holy Week. We meet somewhere in the Salzburg area, at the home of one of the players, who usually invites a fifth, so that each player in turn sits out a hand and merely looks on. (This fifth is often someone hitherto unknown to the others.) On this occasion, the game was to take place in a house on the Mönchsberg, situated, in a manner of speaking, at the bottom of the pass, over which the road, after rising from the plain, leads down to the courtyard of the Festival Theater, and thence to the Old City.

Ever since I was a child, playing cards—and not only the special tarok cards—have for me epitomized "country." That would have been my answer if asked what I visualize when hearing the words "card game." Country in every sense: open country, flat country, countrified country, small country (such as Andorra or San Marino), landlocked country, the country which, unlike the state, has no laws but only customs . . . And, for the adult, cards still have the same magic; they can at any time fit the parts of a country together for him into a whole country. Held fanwise on the four sides of the card table, they represent in my eyes the "heartland," which, as the game proceeds, projects its colors, its smells, and its language beyond the limits of the room into the country round about. Even as a child, when I only watched, every game was for me a kind of circuit, which in the course of the play opened out into a spiral, etc., until the horizon, as I looked out the window, shared in the colors and symbols of the card country. The police siren outside was drawn in, as was the singing of the crazy man in the gateway of the cemetery. During the first card game I was allowed to take part in, a funeral procession came down the street. The feeble-minded woman, who had sometimes let us youngsters look under her skirt, had died. The coffin was draped in white, in token of virginity. It was a day in early January; rain was falling; the trees were black-brown; mole-hills looked out from the yellowish snow. Yes, to me a card game means that country where I, in accordance with my ideal, can show my colors and pledge allegiance to them; above all, where I can be laconic. It needn't absolutely be tarok; just that tarok is probably the most varied, or, as someone once said in the days when it was played more frequently, "the most beautiful of games."

Summer time had been in force for some days. Though the sun was still shining, the supermarket on the ground floor of the apartment house was already closed. The slanting reddish light made the shelves look more spacious. The plastic milk pail—which the old woman, as usual, was carrying on her way to the Moos farm— ordinarily a familiar signal in the dusk, shimmered strangely in the daylight. The houses of the Colony were still half in sunlight, yet the shutters had already been rolled down. Shading his dazzled eyes with one hand, a child appeared at the terrace door in his night-shirt and called out into the garden, where his parents were sitting in strangely premature end-of-the-working-day poses: "I can't sleep." Great flocks of sparrows had taken over the deserted streets and the invitingly vacant bridge. The sun's rays, falling through the slits in the

shutters, covered the newscaster on a television screen
with slanting stripes.

It was too early when I got to the Mönchsberg; the
game was not to begin until nightfall. I might in the
meantime have gone down to the city and read news-
papers in a café. I have often wondered since then why
I didn't give in to my old habit. Be that as it may, I
turned off before reaching the house, and climbed up the
road which, with occasional rises and falls, follows the
long mountain ridge. I didn't turn off as a result of any
decision, yet I thought: "This decides it." All the same,
I insist: I have never questioned the accidental nature of
what I did; I acknowledge it.

With the coming of dusk, the road, which only a short
while before had been intermittently crowded, emptied.
On all sides, what a moment before might have been a
man-made park became a primeval mass of rock.

The ridge of the Mönchsberg is not straight, but re-
capitulates the meanders of the Salzach below. The
mountain consists of the delta rubble deposited by the
river as it emptied into the great lake that was there
thousands of years ago. The rubble was deposited evenly
and rhythmically in layers that can still be discerned
in the slightly tilted striped pattern which runs along
the whole length of the mountain, and is accentuated in
winter by the blown snow in the grooved stripes and by
the serried rows of icicles. The rubble—ranging in content from small pebbles to fist-sized stones—is held together by a light-gray block of limestone which with its
abrupt promontories, needles, sharp edges, and cracks
gives the Mönchsberg its jagged, craglike character.

Where the pebbles have fallen out of the limestone, innumerable craters seem to darken the rock. The layer of humus at the top is thin, and the roots of the trees (for the most part, beeches and oaks) grow right through the often porous shelf of rock below it. In some of the hollows off the main road, there is enough soil for a vegetable garden; but there are also swampy patches that are almost inaccessible. Altogether, the mountain, though wholly surrounded by the city, is not at all a "city mountain"; despite its undeniable urban aspects— benches, blacktop paths, streetlamps—the mountain ridge, once the strollers have gone home, throws one back into the wilderness. Barely a hundred yards below, the city is hidden by fog, while up on the cliff the moon may be shining. The snow that is falling around me at the present moment is rain on the city squares down below a moment later.

If we consider that this mountain owes its origin to a flow of scree into an arm of the delta, might we not speak of its "beginning" and "end"? Thus, I made my way to the end of the mountain, where a flight of stairs, some consisting of old marble, some of new cement (with steps of such varying height that it's easy to lose one's footing on the way down), leads to the Mülln quarter and the Salzach. There on the riverbank is the old people's home, into which I have several times seen men in braided uniforms carrying coffins. Behind it extends the plain, with the new suburbs of Lehen and Liefering; over the football stadium, birds darted to and fro in the glare of the floodlights. Before coming to the stairs, I

turned around and, for fear of being late, took a side
path leading back to the foot of the mountain.

Already the tightly closed lilac buds showed a bluish
shimmer. A big black rag flew into a greening tree: a
raven. The rock was traversed by shiny snail tracks, and
white downy feathers clung to the clefts where bird food
had been strewn. In the midst of bushes and ankle-deep
leaves, a rusty garden gate stood solitary; there was no
fence to go with it, not even a house behind it; it led to
an impassable cliff. Rainwater had gathered in a ring-
shaped beech root, as in a cistern. On a root nearby, a
gray hare was sitting, barely distinguishable from its
resting place; it gave me a friendly look.

Over long, sloping meadows and hollows, the side
path loops back to the ridge road. It starts at the bottom
with another, almost hidden stairway, beside which, in
one of the numerous recesses in the cliff, stands a house
which, though built of stone, looks like a makeshift
shack. It is the meeting place of the local shooting club.
The shooting range is behind the hut, in the wind-
sheltered hollow between the stairs and the cliff, where
under other circumstances the garden would have been
located. Wednesday is crossbow day (as was indicated
by the crossbow emblem flown from the flagpole in front
of the shack). A number of cars were parked in the
driveway, including some from across the border, bear-
ing the insignia of the Berchtesgaden district. At that
moment, a man was removing a dragon-shaped bundle
from the trunk of his car. A signboard attached to a pole
announced a "His-and-Hers Shooting Match," a "Sol-

stice Shooting Match," and a "Fruitcake Shooting Match." All that could be seen of the shooting range from the top of the stairs were the targets; the archers were hidden by a wooden canopy that surrounded the entire range. Each of the targets was lit by a lamp of its own, and the holes in them formed a Braille pattern. Each time a bolt struck home—with a toneless thud—the target and the projectile were carried to the archer on overhead wires and then, minus the bolt, back again. An incessant thudding and whirring could be heard from the brightly lit range, though there was never a human to be seen. On an overhanging cliff behind the hut, there was a doghouse, from which a multiracial mongrel answered the impact of every single bolt with a rather pathetic bark. During a pause in the shooting, conversational voices could be heard. One of the speakers seemed to be a stutterer; when he came to a word beginning with "s," the conversation shifted to the conditional mood—"would have," "would be"—and took a long time getting back to its point of departure, the Singer sewing machine, fustian, worsted, and mother-of-pearl buttons.

On the sloping meadows above the stairs—the archers now inaudible—the densely growing dandelions, interlocking like small cogwheels, had closed with the onset of twilight, and their diurnal yellow gave way to the dark enamel-yellow of the buttercups (more thinly spread, because the flowers were so tiny) on their tall, thin, ramified stems, which, though there was hardly any wind, swayed all along the slope, accentuating the "evening" character of the scene. On this part of the moun-

tain, the rock is almost everywhere covered by grass, but
the green in every rib, bend, groove, and crevice brings
out the rock shapes all the more strikingly. The only
tree on the long slope, almost at the top, is an elder
(ordinarily a mere bush) with a thick trunk, which,
though steeply inclined, is clearly in no danger of
falling. Ring after ring of branches sweep upward in
ever-new impulsions, and the whole tree stands against
the background of the sky as though ready to take off.
In passing, I saw here and there in the forks of the
branches something resembling eyes (just as trees are
improved by having the buds, or "eyes," of other varieties grafted onto them). These were the light-colored
heads of the titmice that spend the night in this elder. As,
climbing higher, I looked back over my shoulder, the
grounds of the provincial hospital came into view. A
white helicopter pattern had been painted on an illuminated circle of concrete, and just then a real helicopter
was landing, while at the edge of the circle an ambulance stood ready, with a stretcher protruding from the
open rear door. Through the great doorway fronting
on the road, a late visitor was stepping out into the
open. In the stairwell of one section, as in certain hotels,
nets were stretched out, which were supposed to stop
patients from jumping over the banisters and into the
lobby. "We wouldn't want to die in there, would we?"
I heard a passerby saying; by then, it had grown so dark
on the mountain that the speaker was faceless.

From here, the slope descends into a deep bowl, suggesting a doline caused by the collapse of an under-
ground cavern. One side of the bowl is almost vertical,

and here the rock, a peculiarity of this bit of meadow, forms a high, naked wall. The bottom of the bowl is sheltered from the wind and the wall is dotted with niches, where the homeless take shelter. In one of these recesses, two figures sat huddled, covered up to their necks with a plastic poncho. A little wood fire lit up their faces. They were a man and a woman, gray-haired and gray-skinned, shoulder to shoulder. There were bottles of liquor on the stone shelf level with their heads, but neither reached for them. They scarcely moved; and when they did move, it was with strange, indecipherable jerks, like creatures out of another geological era. Yet, though they turned not toward each other but toward the fire, they were talking. Noting the observer up at the edge of the bowl, they fell silent and stared at me, motionless, poised for action. They wouldn't do anything, and yet, just with that glance, something had happened between us. Was it only a joke that when I continued on my way a woman coming toward me in the next circle of light cried out: "Help!"

The circle of light did not belong to a streetlamp; it came from the open door of the dormitory at the edge of the clearing; after the vegetable garden behind it, the forest begins again. This dormitory is several stories high; there, at the brow of that primordial hollow, it almost puts one in mind of a skyscraper. Next to it is a smaller service building, with the kitchen and dining room on the ground floor. The path passes between the two buildings. In the dining room, a boy was sitting alone, waiting for his dinner; in the kitchen, a white-clad kitchen maid was ladling soup into his bowl from an enormous caldron. Nearly all the other students must have gone away for the Easter holidays; only a single room in the building was lit; on top of the clothes cupboard, a suitcase; down in the entrance hall, a bicycle with a soccer ball on its baggage rack. The student did not look up when the maid set the soup down in front of him. After the meal, he brought his dishes back to the kitchen and slowly drank a glass of water.

Up on the ridge road, by the streetlamps, I saw two deep-black angled lines on the trunk of a beech tree. They couldn't have been there on my way out; this war paint on the smooth, light-gray bark could not have escaped me. I thought only: Now! Then I bent over, picked up a stone, and set out at a run. Beside a breach in an old battlement, I saw another black spot, even larger than the one on the tree trunk; the paint—I touched it in passing—wasn't dry yet. Could it be that what drove me on was not the fact that they were swastikas? After all, one often comes across swastikas, and not just in this country; and besides, in my excavation work I had seen any number of old artworks in which this symbol has a perfectly innocent meaning or is used as a mere ornament. I recall, for instance, an early Christian mosaic floor in which cranes are carrying swastikas in their beaks. Could, then, this freshly sprayed sign be a symbol of peace? No, a swastika is a swastika. And this sign, this negative image, symbolized the cause of all my melancholy—of all melancholy, ill humor, and false laughter in this country. And this accursed mark had not just been daubed on out of caprice or thoughtlessness; it had been traced with malignant precision and black determination, laid on thickly and thoroughly; the exaggerated hooks were intended to threaten evil, to hit the viewer full in the face; and indeed, they did hit me full in the face. Me? I? One great burst of passion.

In running, I felt an unaccustomed impersonal strength, which, however, did not emanate from the stone in my hand. The very teeth in my mouth became a weapon. On the narrowest part of the mountain, where it tapers down to little more than a crest, a woman in a fur coat was standing by the rail at the edge of the cliff. The streets of the Old City down below were recognizable only by the narrow, reddish trails of light between the dark, almost deserted buildings. In the darkness, the illumined twin steeples of the Kollegienkirche, which, with the rings of light-colored stone figures on their flat roofs, resemble castles on a chessboard by day, became grimacing Indian idols; the clocks became eye sockets, the window ledges bulging foreheads, and the rings of statues flaming hair. The most tranquil and at the same time the most powerful lights in the city were the rows of reddish-yellow lamps on the railroad-station platforms. Reflected in the water, the cars on the river bridges became vastly magnified shadow caravans without beginning or end. Two crossed overhead bus wires hissed like a whiplash through the deserted city squares.

Nothing escaped my notice as I ran. In passing, I kicked a paper carton with some French-fried potatoes left in it off the path (a McDonald's has recently opened on Getreidegasse, the Old City Commission has commended its façade for blending harmoniously with the neighboring buildings; a lot of the young people, including my children, meet there). A hedgehog, dark legs, black snout, shining little eyes, dug itself out of a pile of leaves—no doubt it had just awakened from its winter sleep—and then swam seal-like through the mass of foliage, heading for the woods. In places, especially noticeable to the runner, the mountaintop was immersed in exhaust fumes from the ventilation shafts of the garages built into the rock below. On a dwarf tree, a mere pole split down the middle, sat an enormous owl, within reach of the road; it did not take flight at my approach, but fluffed up its feathers, turned its head toward me, and followed me with its round eyes.

At its apex, the road passes between two long walls of rock. At one point, the gully thus formed was not "empty," or so it seemed to me as I ran. My eye fell first on a spray can (the word "bomb" rose to my mind), then on the finger on the button, and last on the figure attached to it. The figure had no contours, but immediately had a name: the name given, in a purportedly faithful Bible translation, to "the evil one"—the Frustator. Time and again, one meets with hostile faces, but the Frustator, the archenemy, is faceless. Up until then, I had often had intimations of his presence, though always in a crowd, in passing: a grotesquely supple thumb joint; the chalk-white interior of a mouth; a bare foot shaped like a crocodile; an eye from which all color seemed to have drained; a neck swollen from blowing into a police whistle. But here at last I saw him as a whole, not in a crowd, but alone.

The runner became a pursuer and pursuit meant "action." No such thought as "I shouldn't" or "I have no right" entered his head; at the most: "For my own good, I had better . . ." Perhaps, in spite of everything, I'd have run past him if he hadn't been standing in the middle of the road. But then the stone was thrown and the enemy lay literally crushed on the ground, as unexpectedly as once in my childhood a rooster which, unintentionally to be sure, I had hit on the head with a pebble thrown from a distance—with the sole difference that the rooster, just as surprisingly, stood up and ran off as if nothing had happened.

I had not thrown blindly, but with wide-open eyes; I had not seen my surroundings but, strangely enough, larger-than-life, my own face. It looked to me neither grimacing nor calm; it looked more like the face of an unknown person, or rather of a hitherto unknown, close relative, who had now at last turned up.

Though I did not regard my adversary as an animal, another incident involving an animal comes to mind. Some children were throwing stones at a cat, saying: "If we hit it, we aimed wrong." I had not aimed wrong. Even as, still running, I pulled back for the throw, I knew my stone would strike home—and kill.

A wind came up. As so often on this mountain island, the wind was suddenly there, without preceding squalls. It blew in full force, as though its passage through the Bavarian plains had been a buildup and this point on the fringe of the Alps its goal. The sounds of the immediate vicinity, clearly audible only a short moment before, were gone. But the roaring of the wind brought the slightest, most distant noises close. A board fell to

the ground. A horse neighed. Someone stood outside
a house and laughed. A hammerblow was followed by
the clanking of an oil drum. A bell note came from one
of the churches on the edge of the city (or in one of the
villages beyond). And perhaps that clapping of hands
was far outside the city limits.

With great groaning wings a swan, white in the darkness, flew over the mountain. The wind was cold and
brought with it a mass of clouds that scudded across the
sky with the speed of a spring tide. Briefly, the moon
peered out of the advancing veil of mist, and then was
seen no more. The swaying trees on the ridge made the
strings of lights on the plain below flicker and tremble.
The treetops roared like a squadron of planes. Above
them, there was not a star to be seen; only a blinking
satellite flashed for a moment across a last hole in the
clouds. The leaf buds seemed to have blown off the
trees, leaving a dead forest of swaying crags; the clumps
of mistletoe in the branches were abandoned birds' nests.
The mountain was now inaccessible; and yet, wide open
to nature's grandeur, I thought: This is the world! Together with the beaklike shells of the empty beechnuts
above me, the lights on the plain below were its capital
city.

I bent over the dying man. He puffed out his cheeks,
as though gill-breathing had set in. From his breast
pocket emerged, scarcely audible, music from a tiny
transistor radio. The man was wearing checked knee
socks, and his coat had light-colored patches at the
elbows, which reminded me of certain armbands. He
seemed elderly; his hair was white. Or could it be that

he was really young and had only now, by a speed-up
process as in time-lapse photography, become white-
haired and wrinkled? I experienced a strange disgust—
a kind of sympathy with this man's disgust at having to
die; at having lost his Christian name and being reduced
to some sort of "dead Otto" or "dead Erwin." Then the
white-haired man actually made a grimace of extreme
revulsion, which spread to me as I bent over him.

With this grimace still on my face, I quickly dragged
the body out of the road and up the embankment. At this
point the edge of the cliff is near, and I let the dead man
fall. I was pulled after him, and for a moment I fell
with him.

Sometimes the suicides who jump off this mountain
fall through the roofs of houses down below or tear the
overhead wires of the bus line. But this side of the mountain did not overlook the city; it surmounted seldom fre-
quented terraces and obscure patches of woods. This
incident—I knew while the body was falling—would
never be cleared up. My freedom was not threatened.
The body would quietly rot. And nevertheless, since I
had thrown that stone (of this, too, I was certain), action
against me was underway—not a legal proceeding, not
an inquest; not a demand for extradition; but—at last
I found the word which restored my lucidity—a "challenge."

Back in the gully, I picked up my projectile, which
was still lying there, and with it scraped the unfinished
rune off the rock. The stone grew hot in my hand from
the friction and smelled like a flint just before the sparks
fly. I sat down on a tree root protruding, at the height

of a folding chair, from the opposite wall, close to the scene of the crime. At this point, there is a double bend in the road; this gave me a view of a separate section of the rock face, shaped like a truncated pyramid and topped like a ruin with grass and saplings. Here for the moment lay the ruins of a temple in the jungles of Central America. Then in the lamplight the cliff took on the gray coloration of a wasp's nest, riddled with black cells which seemed abandoned yet alive. The layer of foliage at the foot of the cliff blew back and forth in the storm wind, with eddies, waterspouts, and breakers, and the nest with its black holes changed into a chalk-white oyster bed (the oysters being the shell-shaped stones protruding from the cliff). At the center of the oyster bed, the symbol I had scraped away marked an empty space which, as I saw it, belonged to the cranes, the gulls, and the kingfishers of the silent world. And I experienced a sense of triumph at having killed. I even smacked my lips aloud. This is my history now, I thought. My history will sustain me. Justice had been done, and I belonged to the nation of criminals; no nation is more dispersed and isolated.

It was a big mountain. No blood would flow from the city fountains. No animal would talk. "Everybody off this mountain!" (I shouted that.) Only then did it come to me that I had cursed the dying man in his last moment and hurled the same curse after the corpse as it fell off the cliff. And my obituary was as follows: "At last, you have lost your right to exist!"

At the far end of the gully, a female jogger appeared, not detracting from the emptiness but enhancing it. She was embodied beauty, with blond hair and a jogging suit that glowed fire-hydrant blue in the darkness. In hurrying past, she smiled at the figure sitting on the tree root, and I smiled back. "Marvelous evening, isn't it?" "Yes, today this gully is eternal." As she ran, she played with the fingers of her striped gloves as with puppets. Punch and Judy teetered, jumped up, collapsed, flailed out at each other, and hugged, keeping up a dialogue all the while. A spotted cat came running after the jogger, pursued by a single tiny beech leaf scurrying over the ground.

When I stood up, I was so unexpectedly tired that I could hardly move. It wasn't far to my card game (wasn't I hours late already?), but I'd never get there. Something drew me off the road, into a nook to sleep in. When at last I moved, it was blindly, with my eyes shut. I didn't even look when something came panting up behind me (a group of joggers). Blindly I groped my way over the meandering road, as though following the canal down below. When my eyes finally opened, what they saw, looking extraordinarily substantial, were a street sweeper's twig broom leaning against a gravel box and, as though lit by the brightest sun, the white, granular wall with its lighted windows. "Here I am." Who said that to whom?

The other card players were a priest, a young politician, a painter, and the master of the house. They were sitting in the library, a room almost bare except for books. The knotholes in the wide floorboards seemed at first sight to move in the cigar smoke. The legs of the light maplewood table, as the priest explained in the pause produced by my arrival, formed a St. Andrew's cross, so called after the apostle Andrew, who had suffered martyrdom on an X-shaped cross. The name Andreas—which happens to be mine—aroused laughter and led quite naturally to my joining in the game. As if I hadn't been late at all, I sat at the table, fanning out my cards.

Before that, I had stood a while on the threshold of the house. This threshold consisted of round stakes of varying thicknesses, each with its specific annual rings, pounded up to their heads into the ground, the whole giving the impression of interlocking wheels, or rather, because of the radial cracks in the wood, of juxtaposed sun disks, framed on the right and left by the dark green lanceolate tips of oleander bushes. Threshold and oleander were lit by a spotlight affixed to the lintel, as an indication that this was the scene of the card game. "Threshold, play on," read the old-fashioned writing on the door. And: "Card game, lead us."

A few of the painter's pictures hung on the windowside wall, where there were no books. Unframed and unglassed, they seemed to be emanations of the wall itself. A rust-brown, a saltpeter-gray, a mold-silver, a brick-red, a resin-yellow. Unlike other pictures, they did not draw the eye to a point but merely reflected colors. These, said the painter, "should be as luminous as the colors in a stained-glass window; that is my ideal." Though he had lived in the city a long time, he was the stranger to the group. His eyes were invisible, so deeply embedded that their sockets rather resembled the eye-

holes in a mask. Sometimes his voice was like that of a
child, soft and matter-of-fact; and he never had to clear
his throat before starting to speak. He kept holding up
the game by discovering in each card dealt him a certain
color providing the basis for a lengthy discussion. (Or
he would bend down to the carpet and appear to be
rubbing its wine red and cobalt blue into his face as a
kind of war paint.) He was so short that his head barely
rose above the edge of the table. He always stood up to
deal. His tricks had to be pushed over to him.

The stairwell had smelled of apples, as strongly as a
fruit cellar. The aroma was lost in the room where we
were playing but became all the more pungent if one
stepped outside. At times, moreover, one caught a whiff,
though through a barrier of baffling admixtures, of spices
from the food simmering in the kitchen below, to which
our host turned his attention whenever he was out of the
game: thyme? savory? cinnamon? Once, when the window was opened for a moment, someone was heard to
say: "You can smell the snow he predicted." "He" was
the weather broadcaster.

The house was not quiet. Time and again, steps were
heard on the winding stairs which led not only to the
library but also to the various bedrooms; among them
a swift, light scurrying as of an animal's paws. Then
there was a scratching at the outside door, and someone
admitted a cat, which lay under the table during the
rest of the game. It had a dark head, with yellow eyes;
when the eyes were closed, the whole head was black.

In a basement room, a cello was being played, a
heavy, long-drawn-out rumbling, which, in a manner of

speaking, gave the whole house a musical foundation. The cello notes made the time pass more slowly; almost everyone who went by the house stopped to listen; and sometimes the players inside suspended their movements, as though for them, under the spell of Orpheus' voice, things had stopped moving for a while. At the same time it was ship's music; the library with its paneled ceiling was the salon, and the little oval windows in the gable were the portholes.

The cello fell silent. A bottle of wine was uncorked. The telephone rang in the entrance hall ("Not for me," said the master of the house, while someone who could not have been an adult ran down the stairs). In the dark garden, the evergreen leaves of a holly tree glistened; the dull-black shape in it was a sleeping blackbird. A single stone lion, no larger than a hare, crouched on a pedestal near the garden gate. Down in the city, people were besieging the one open shop where cigarettes and news-papers were available. The trains at the railroad station looked colorful and massive, like components of the big cities they had come from or were going to; the tracks were a recumbent pyramid. And far from the station, the broken bottles atop the prison wall suggested pyramids of a very different kind.

Our game on the mountainside was fitful. If one player let his thoughts wander, did that suffice to make the others lose interest? Yet we were all serious about the game. I had seldom played so resolutely and I per-sisted in playing every hand. But there was no joy in it; only a dogged determination to win. And we couldn't stop. Instead of becoming, as usual, more intimate as the game went on, we became more estranged. None of us could look his partner in the eye. We observed the rules punctiliously, yet our looks and gestures were those of cheats; and to cheat in this way is to play at playing. A lost feeling came over us. We all felt out of place. And in the place where we should have been long ago, "everything was too late." On the one hand, five lost card players were on the verge of tears; on the other hand, each went on doing, and overdoing, his own thing: the master of the house kept pouring more wine; the painter, at every glance, discovered and exclaimed about some new color in the room (for instance, those spots of mold on the spine of a book); and the priest, in his capacity as a recognized authority on tarok, author of a treatise on the history of the game in the various countries of Europe, surprised the company by invoking weird and unusual exceptions and sub-exceptions to the rules (though these did not always work in his favor).

Only the politician tried, so to speak, to make the wind change. He proceeded as though he were responsible for the evening, which for him was not just another evening but a time of testing. Especially in his leisure hours, he always felt called upon to prove himself, to show that he could handle any situation. He would jump at the slightest opportunity to demonstrate his capacity for immediate action. If a mouse was sighted, he was the one to wake the sleeping cat and put it on the scent; if a glass fell to the floor, he would instantly block off the disaster zone where splinters threatened—and signal like a traffic cop to the person who arrived with dustpan

and brush. Where others were panicked or hesitant, he
was in his element. At present, to be sure, his determination that every moment should demonstrate his leader-
ship, energy, and competence only made matters worse.
He spoke and moved as though trying to take charge in
an overcrowded lifeboat: with an enormous display of
muscle, he tries to start the dead engine, and succeeds
only in flooding it, while at the same time belaboring
the faces and bellies of those to the right and left of him
with his elbows, until, with all the fumbling and floun-
dering, the boat threatens to capsize. To reconcile the
players, he looked for resemblances. For instance, he
found a resemblance in the way the master of the house
and the painter put their glasses down after every sip;
he discovered that the eyeglasses of the priest and of
the master of the house were the same strength; and I,
"the teacher," had in common with him, the politician,
if not his political party, at least the habit of pounding
my cards with my fist instead of picking them up.

But the politician himself was lost, and more visibly
than the rest of us, with eyes agape and beads of sweat
on his hairline. The worst of it was that he refused to
acknowledge his inability to cope with the situation, and
kept on trying. Yet it was just this that brought the others
together! While, a moment before, they had been staring
into space, they now exchanged covert glances and even
smiles, and stretched out their legs under the table
in relief. Nothing was lacking but the one word that
would have saved the day. But then, quite inexplicably,
salvation came, brought by someone's casual remark
about the coming of Easter: "In three days, the bells

will ring again." That was the turning point. With a sense of release, we played a last hand and went downstairs to the dining room for dinner.

After the meal, the master of the house suggested making a fire in the fireplace, and each of the card players wanted to light it. The almost white beech logs lay in a disorderly pile in the wide entrance hall. One player after another carried a few of them in and put them down near the fireplace. All this time, a teenager, the son of our host, was standing outside at the hall telephone, with his back to the wood carriers, pressing the phone to his ear without so much as a glance at all the disturbance. ("It's been going on like this since the beginning of his vacation," said the boy's father.)

The table had been cleared, the door was closed, the fire was burning, the card players sat drinking wine, the predicted snow ("the last snow," someone said) came flying out of the darkness and beat against the windowpanes, which crackled at first, then were silent, as though a tension in the glass had been relieved; the son in the hallway kept mumbling into the telephone. Each one of the downward-swarming snowflakes was a symbol, undefined and undefinable.

I tapped my temples with my fingertips, as though to relieve some pressure or pain, pushed back my chair, and turned to the priest: "Do thresholds occur in the religious tradition?" I asked him. —"Literally or figuratively?" —"Both."

While the priest pondered, the others said whatever came into their heads.

The master of the house: "Our cat here never runs

thoughtlessly over a threshold. It always stops first and carefully sniffs the ground. Sometimes it avoids contact with the threshold and jumps. It's only when escaping from a dog, for instance, that it loses no time in crossing a threshold; all it wants is to be inside. Then of course it's the pursuer that hesitates."

The politician: "I have two sorts of recurrent dreams about thresholds. In the first, I'm in my stocking feet; I slide off the threshold because, regardless of whether it's wood or stone, it's exceedingly smooth and rounded at the edges. But I always get to the other side safely, and my fear helps me. In sliding off, I ask myself: Where am I? And precisely because of my fright, I know where I am. In this case, the threshold is something like the take-off board in the broad jump. In the other sort of dream, it's just the threshold of a room, a mere strip of metal such as you often find in new buildings. But I'm incapable of crossing it. In the whole dream, nothing happens, just that I'm standing by the open door, looking at my face, which is reflected in the metal under me. Once, when I managed to turn around, I saw behind me a glass cage full of simultaneous interpreters, all waiting for me to start making my speech."

The painter: "Two ancient peoples were such bitter enemies that when one had defeated the other, it smashed the statues in the other's temples and used the stone for paving its thresholds at home. In some cultures, we find labyrinth designs outside the thresholds; their purpose, we are told, is not so much to protect the threshold as to make intruders stop and consider a detour. To me personally, thresholds are no problem. I'm not mature enough for that. Nevertheless, I've sometimes thought: If there are paintings over doorframes, why not build thresholds and make them more recognizable by means of colored forms? We'll see."

By then, the priest had collected his thoughts. "To the best of my knowledge," he said, "the tradition has little to say of the threshold as a material object. One of the prophets predicts that the temple will tremble so violently that even its stone threshold will be lifted. As an image, however, it occurs time and again, though as a rule a different word is used. In the indexes of works on the subject, *threshold* usually refers us to *door*. The threshold and the door (or gate) are seen as parts standing for the whole. In the Old Testament, the whole is the city: in one passage, the mere earthly city— 'Howl, O gate; cry, O city!'; in another, the heavenly city—'The Lord loveth the gates of Zion more than all the dwellings of Jacob.' In the New Testament, the gate stands in one passage for perdition—'the gates of hell'; in another, for salvation—'I am the door: by me if any man enter in, he shall be saved.' Thus, the threshold is ordinarily associated with passage from one zone to another. What may be less evident is that the threshold is itself a zone, or rather, a place in its own right, a place of testing or of safety. Isn't the ash heap where Job sits in his misery a threshold, a place of testing? Didn't a fugitive put himself under someone's protection by sitting down on his threshold? Doesn't the archaic usage of 'gate' evoke the threshold as a dwelling place, as a room in its own right? According to modern doctrine, of course, there are no longer any thresholds in this sense. The only threshold still remaining to us, says one of our modern teachers, is that between waking and dreaming, and nowadays little attention is paid to that. Only in the insane does it protrude, visible to all, into daytime experience, like the fragments of the destroyed temples just mentioned. For a threshold, he says, is not a boundary—boundaries are on the increase both in inner and in outer life—but a precinct. The word 'threshold' embraces transformation, floor, river crossing, mountain pass, enclosure (place of refuge). According to an almost forgotten proverb: 'The threshold is a fountainhead.' And this teacher says literally: 'It was from thresholds that lovers and friends absorbed strength. But,' he goes on, 'where nowadays are we to find the destroyed thresholds, if not in ourselves? By our own wounds shall we be healed. If snow stops falling from the clouds, let it continue to fall inside me.' Every step, every glance, every gesture, says the teacher, should be aware of itself as a possible threshold and thus recreate what has been lost. This new threshold consciousness might then transfer attention from object to object, and so on until the peace relay reappears on earth, at least on that one day—and on the day after and the day after that, rather as in the child's game where stone sharpens scissors, scissors cut paper, and paper wraps stone. Thus, thresholds as seats of power may not have disappeared; they have become conceivable, so to speak, as inner powers. If man were conscious of these thresholds, he would at least let his fellow man die a natural death. Threshold consciousness is nature religion. More cannot be promised."

The priest pulled himself up in his chair and looked around, as though preparing to go on with his sermon, but then laughed as though surprised, exhaled, inhaled deeply, and told us how he had just remembered the stone threshold at home, on which he had often sat "bare-assed." This threshold had been a granite block, not in the house but in the wooden barn. The threshold of the house was a simple pinewood board with an unusually deep knothole in it; he and his brothers and sisters had often sat there playing marbles in rainy weather. They had sometimes scraped their fingers on the rough board or got them full of splinters, which later festered.

His listeners also recalled things that had happened long ago. When one stopped, another took over, and the result was a single story in many voices.

"Sitting on the doorstep had a Sunday, end-of-the-day quality. A duty had been done and now you were resting. When passersby saw someone sitting this way on his doorstep, they became friendly. He was in his right place. Once, when some bigger children were chasing me with sticks, I didn't run into the house, I waited for them on the threshold; they greeted me and nodded as if nothing had happened. Some thresholds were very high; in crossing them, you lifted your knees and bumped your head on the doorframe. Sitting on the threshold meant that the door could not be closed. Of course there wasn't much you could do; at the most, blow soap bubbles or read, propping your heels and shoulders on the doorframe. The women would set a chair on the threshold and sit there with their knitting. I often used to stand on the threshold, watching a storm and letting the raindrops or a stray hailstone graze me. Once, when my grandmother had an attack of asthma, she ran out of the house and stood on the threshold screaming with terror and gagging (in the end, her screams were no more than squeaks). Some mornings, there were dead mice and birds' feathers on the threshold, matted with blobs of innards. At spring-cleaning time, the thresholds got a thorough scrubbing; warm steam rose up from them, they showed their original pattern and smelled good. At Whitsuntide the thresholds were made festive with birch saplings on either side. I thought the threshold of my parents' room was especially high. Strange signs were incised in the threshold of the house next door; it had formerly been a tombstone. The village wisdom had it that in case of earthquake you should not run out into the open but stand on the threshold under the doorframe; there you were safe. For me, 'threshold' evoked 'ripping up'; because it was always the wood of the threshold that was first attacked by mold and that had to be replaced most frequently. Thresholds are noticed only in the country; in the city, they are forgotten. The most beautiful threshold I've ever seen was a natural creation, the entrance to a stalactite cave; it was a compact, luminous slab, perfectly rounded, an additional glassy-white floor among floors. The most beautiful threshold *I* ever saw was a kitchen threshold, covered with linoleum and riddled with thumbtacks; after a day of talk, I had come home to palpable things; the threshold is my place, I thought, and there I stood. Standing outside a closed door as a child, I would shout 'Stupid pup!' instead of 'Open up!'

And similarly, at the threshold of the forest, I'd shout 'Stupid pup!' before going in. Bird tracks on the snow-covered threshold. What is the opposite of threshold phobia? Fringe benefit."

The others turned to the questioner. Had he wanted to "test" us? He replied: "No, not test, just make you tell stories. You see, I've noticed that there's no better way of getting people to tell stories than to ask them about thresholds." In the enthusiasm of our storytelling, we even interrupted the son of the house, who was still on the telephone, to ask him what he thought a threshold was. He answered succinctly: "A nuisance!" and sank back into his telephone corner.

One after another fell silent. But this was not the usual lull in the conversation before a group breaks up. The storytelling seemed, rather, to continue in the silence, and thus to become more eloquent than ever. Each of us delved deeper into himself and there met his neighbor, with whom he now, without trying, had everything in common. "Once upon a time there was we." (How is it that I can say "we"? After all, we were not very many. And I trusted this "we." Once upon a time there was a fact.) One burst out laughing, seemingly out of a clear sky, and another nodded; or one drew a line through a ring of wine on the table, and his neighbor added to it.

We had stopped drinking; our host forgot to pour more wine and the guests forgot to empty their glasses. Cigars went out and so did pipes. A smell of quinces drifted in; and, from outside, puffs of snowy air. Our host stopped being a host; from then on, he was merely one of the several persons who had met "somewhere." We all sat straight in our chairs, as though backrests were no longer needed. Were we waiting for something? No, the event—the story—had already happened. In the embers of the dying fire, our collective eye discerned a glittering nocturnal metropolis filled with roaring, flashing, and crashing, with relays of light and shadow running from end to end; sometimes sparks shot across it like ambulances. Strange how the gaze sinks into fire, whereas it usually bounces back from flowing water.

We were not waiting; yet someone was still missing. We didn't know it until the lady of the house, just back from somewhere, appeared in a festive midnight-blue coat and boots shaped like birds' beaks, and sat down nonchalantly in our midst. She completed the circle. Beside her the men looked unshaven, and beside them the woman's face, shaded by a broad-brimmed hat, betrayed a fatigue that was a kind of happiness. Something had moved her (a musical phrase? the snowy night?). Quite naturally, she took part in the silent, all-disentangling exchange of stories. In the midst of the warm room, her coat gave off cold; the snow crystals on it, interlocking at first, softened visibly into drops of water. A daddy longlegs ran into our field of vision, its little round body duplicated by the shadow under it. Outside the window, a screech owl, so close it might have been perched on the windowsill, let out a catlike screech. The house next door became visible, a yellow wall covered by a wisteria vine, its arm-thick stem coiled and tangled like a display of sailor's knots. A birch stood white in the darkness, its hanging switches moved only by the falling snow, only one branch vibrating in the void; a bird must have just landed on it. A yew tree grew star-shaped out of the ground, its star-shaped needles pointing like a road sign to the arch in the hollow, which framed the sparse but brightly twinkling lights on the plain below.

We separated outside the house, where the road branches off in different directions. The snow along the edges (it had melted everywhere else, except in the half-rolled leaves of a box tree, the whole of which it trans-formed into a snowy beacon) heightened the "cross-roads" image. Each went his own way. Our host walked backward through the front garden to the house. His wife stood upstairs in the open window, looking out beyond us; her charm was of the kind that made one dream and not stare. For a moment, the house—the lantern affixed to the outside wall made you think of a farmyard at night—seemed to be part of a mountain village.

Instead of heading across the plain on my way home, I turned into a street so narrow that no one could have walked beside me. This street describes a loop which, after a steep hill, leads to the main road to the Old City. A phone rang in a house on the hill just once, as if it were a signal. I wanted to be alone with the falling snow. As I went downhill, something drew me upward, but to a much higher mountain, above the tree line; in my thoughts I saw myself on the crest of the Untersberg

at night, between bare limestone cliffs, with nothing on
my mind but the next step and the next handhold:
"wholly present!"

Down at the intersection I ran into the painter, who
was deep in contemplation of a cleft in the rock that was
covered by a climbing plant—not just covered, but completely filled with it; he was holding a heavy robe of
tight-meshed blossoms, blue through and through,
bedded and framed in leaves. In the blowing, melting,
then freezing snow the blue had the color of an old
glacier; the flowery train was its tongue. When I looked
longer, the blue seemed to stand out against it, and an
expression often heard at digs came to my mind: "You
must find the edges." The painter swung the plant-robe
and called out to me: "How merry are colors in motion!" And: "There are colors everywhere!" And:
"Colors need to act!"

Together we went down the so-called Festival Stairway.
On the last step the painter stopped, pointed one hand
at the mountain behind us and the other at the Festival
buildings ahead of us, and said: "It's not a threshold
that made me stop here. No, what stops me is a borderline. Or rather: something in me is stopped here, even if
I go on. When I set foot in the Old City, something in
me stops breathing. Some say the city puts them in a
bad mood. I call that an understatement. A bad mood
that makes you scream is more like pain. Whenever I
come here, I try to pretend that nothing is wrong. But
after a few steps, the borderline makes itself felt, colors
lose their meaning, and even if I run, I can't breathe.
And the main thing perhaps is not the crowding—now,

for instance, the city is empty—but this overpowering central zone that no crowd can fill. Or is it the other way around, that nothing can fill the center, so that all there can be is a disorderly crowd—a pushing, staggering, shoving, a barring the way to one another, as nowhere else in the world? No, nothing here makes for space, neither the parades nor the march-pasts of scarfaced city officials nor the swaying chamois beards on simpletons' hats. Nor the processions of glittering brocade cloaks and golden monstrances; nor the melancholy idlers. And yet I once saw a procession in the city: a group of feebleminded people, slapping each other on the back, pushing and wrestling, swarming from souvenir shop to souvenir shop, shouting their joy at being let out, at being in town. The big bells, it's true, give one a feeling of the place, except for the chimes, which to my mind evoke the slamming of a tin door, a car that won't start, someone clearing his throat, or the clatter of high-heeled shoes. Did you ever lose your footing in the woods, while climbing a mountain for instance, and reach through the underbrush to grab a rotting tree trunk? Precisely because your hand meets with no resistance, you feel for a moment as if it were gone (severed by a yellow and black salamander or some other crawling thing). I've often had a comparable feeling when coming into this city. Here, too, the transitions are as camouflaged as the boundary between mold and foliage. See how the façade of the Festival Theater in front of us has been adapted to the mountain behind us? In the eyes of those responsible for the building, the gravel embedded in the limestone makes the mountain-

side look like concrete; and that was their justification
for building with concrete. They even prided themselves
on the idea: mountain and theater were one. To make
the building even more mountainlike, they chiseled artificial fissures into its concrete façade. That's what I
mean by border fraud. And I call it a crime. Take a
look at the line back there, where the rock face seems to
merge with the concrete. At first sight, the two sub-
stances that have been forced together don't even seem
related; in the mountain, you see any number of oblique
layers, and in each layer, after you've looked at it for a
while, the sinking, rolling, stopping, and spreading of
gravel is repeated, along with the intervals when the
waters were at rest. With each new stripe, the tide seems
to change. But in the adjacent concrete wall, the most
you can detect is the impetus with which at some time or
other—you get no feeling of time—a mixture of cement
and gravel was poured into the revetment. The rock is
covered with moss and lichen, its recesses and outcrop-
pings with flowers and grass; the imitation, on the other
hand, is covered with a film of cement, and not so much
as a blade of grass has ever grown in its artificial fissures. How colorful the mountain can be, especially in
wet weather; apparent gray turns to brown, yellow and
red, even eggshell white, basalt black and bottle green,
after the manner of gravel paths in the rain—whereas
this monstrosity thrown up in front of it shimmers
eternally in its pallid non-color. Isn't it strange? The
mountain, a piece of nature, is real to us, whereas the
artifact affecting kinship with it repels us with its
ludicrous unreality. Border fraud is in this case a crime,

and such criminals are my enemies. Even on the mountain slopes, criminals erect their bastions with impunity: they need only leave the façades of their residential or commercial bunkers unfinished and they are given credit for respecting the environment. Any sheet-metal shack, any space station, any Bedouin's tent would be more respectful. And the disrespect so typical of our city is most strikingly exemplified in the Festival Stairway, on the bottommost step of which we are now standing; which the experts rave about; and which in my opinion is of all outdoor stairways in the world the least deserving of the name. Ordinarily the word 'stairway' makes me think of 'airiness'; here I think of 'doldrums.' The mustiness of the whole city begins at the uppermost landing. Here again, on these stairs, there is no space. Hardly anyone lingers here. At the most, someone wanting to catch his breath will lean on the iron bar that has been cemented onto the concrete in lieu of a banister. On the way down, a lot of people run; on the way up, they count the steps either aloud or to themselves, as one might in a tower. The steps—split granite slabs—are too high, too narrow, and too shallow. Footfalls are dull thuds or squeaks; you can't walk two abreast if someone is coming in the opposite direction; if two people do walk side by side, the steepness makes their conversation shrill and it's frequently interrupted by panting; when I meet my best friend here, we hardly recognize each other because the difference in elevation distorts our faces—and often enough they are not just distorted but also obscured by a shimmering film of cement—or else I see him only as a silhouette, it's as if I were seeing him at the far end of a tunnel. These stairs don't leap up the mountainside as an independent structure, they are a mere accessory of the concrete, which in places they are obliged to tunnel under. Instead of sweeping lines, they move in sharp angles followed by sudden curves, which are as troublesome to a slow walker as to a runner. The middle landing, which in other stairways offers an occasion to stop and look around, is placed in a dark and musty tunnel with a black puddle of urine in one corner and a pile of black-and-white pigeon droppings in the other. No, this isn't an outdoor stairway; it's a sewer. The *Magic Flute* serpent hewn into the stone parapet isn't an ornament, it's just bric-a-brac, and the court at the lower end of the sewer is likewise full of Festival bric-a-brac, and other kinds as well. And I must beg you not to imagine that my nocturnal tirade is my last word about border fraud. I mean to . . ."

The painter stopped and laughed. "Hm. What *will* I do? What will we do? Because my enemies elude my enmity."

He stepped down from the stairs to city level and continued: "One day, when passing the statue of Mozart, I was surprised for a moment to notice that the face is turned toward the Old City. I had always thought of it as looking toward the river and away from the city. Then another day I was surprised to see that the two Gorgons' heads to the right and left of the New Gate— the real mountain tunnel—point the way out of the city; I had always thought that the snakes in their hair and their blood-curdling eyes were addressed, rather, toward people going into the city."

We went from one Old City square to another: all deserted, except for one where a drunk was leaning against the fountain, asleep; he was clutching a bottle, and one of his cheeks was puffed up. But the bars were loud with what the painter called the laughter of "triumphant heartlessness." At that point, to my own surprise, I managed a reply of sorts.

"But," I said, "would the light and air beyond the borderlines you speak of be so effective, so refreshing, so substantial if not for the dead calm in the center? Without it, would I, in passing from the Old City to the plain, always be overwhelmed by a wave of space? When I stay away from the city, the wave fails me. Doesn't this suggest that the one sphere makes the other possible? And what better example can there be of how emptiness and superabundance complement each other? I, in any case, need the city and I need it as it is. My place is the center; it, too, takes its measure from outside, from the plain, and then I am its master. Every swarm of tourists that bars my way is welcome to me. The circle I describe around camera-toters starts me on my way to the open meadows; every detour I make in the crowd brightens the country daylight for me. The poet Georg Trakl, who celebrated the 'beautiful city'—didn't they all go strolling on the empty plain almost every day? Maybe it's just that Salzburg should have another name: Charleroi or Taranto, or in a pinch Salinas? Yet salt was once held sacred. It transformed the stranger into an honored guest. Look at a handful of salt crystals under a magnifying glass; those translucent cubes glitter like the walls of a white city, with the crystals strewn farthest from the center as its outworks. Salt is dear to me—to look at, to touch, to season with. It reminds me of my birth and embodies a kind of measure, or law. Once in a Mediterranean salt marsh I saw the 'house where it was born,' a stone building on a jetty far out in the water, with an outdoor stairway leading to the entrance on the upper story. In Virgil, salt is always connected with the words 'small' and 'concealed.' This salt house seemed small and its inhabitants, or so at least I thought, lived in concealment."

We had stopped at the end of the Mozart Footbridge across the Salzach. At that point the painter asked me my name, which, he said, he hadn't caught when we were introduced. Then a strange thing happened; without a moment's hesitation, I said my name was Hurler, and even added: "No, I'm not joking, that's my real name— Hurler."

The painter answered in a tone of friendly mockery: "Judging by what you've just been saying, it ought to be Spite." Thereupon he set foot on the wooden bridge. As I remained on the bank below, his eyes were now level with mine. His way of taking leave was to observe that my face reminded him of the boisterous idiots whose forays through the city he would so gladly have joined: "They were my family." Then he vanished across the bridge. Once, from halfway across, he called back that he wished for my sake that this night's snow would turn to salt. Reclusive as I was, I then learned something: to look back—the backward glance, as it were.

The footbridge remained deserted. Just once, a couple appeared, the woman wearing a long evening dress under her fur coat, followed by a little girl with braces on her teeth, pushing a bicycle. Under her footsteps, the bridge swayed like a gangplank. The entrance to the bridge with its crossbars looked like a gangway that would be lifted as soon as these people had passed; then no one would be able to board the ship.

The squat, mottled trunks of plane trees came into sight on the opposite bank, lighting up that whole part of the city. On the hither side, brownish slush was splattered by cars, in whose dark interior a white shirt collar could now and then be seen. Accentuated by the swarms of snowflakes, the headlight beams of cars moving bumper to bumper looked like towropes. Here by the side of the shore road, the victim of a traffic accident had once lain, whimpering, clutching his legs to his belly, foaming at the mouth, his teeth chattering; mistaken at first for a "victim" in a first-aid exercise. The swollen but almost soundless river carried whole green bushes along with it. Not a single bell was ringing. In an isolated house on the slope of the Kapuzinerberg, the lights went out one by one. An alarm clock ticked; an ink pad dried. It came to my mind that the name of the road I was standing on was masculine and that of the one on the opposite shore feminine: Rudolfskai and Giselakai. The deserted footbridge was framed on both sides by an iron structure which crossed the river in three arches, hop skip jump. The entrance to the bridge was an arcade, decorated with a climbing plant that made me think of Virgil's "smiling" acanthus. Here, however, nothing smiled. The bridge gave off the wrong emptiness, not the kind I wanted. For a while, I inwardly kept up my conversation with the painter, at first so intensely that I accompanied it with gestures; then my arms hung motionless and my silent monologue died away. A whiff of perfume came to me from the arcade—from the woman in the evening dress?—and the melting snow dripped and gurgled in the drains. I had had epaulettes of snow, which now quickly vanished.

Though there was plenty of room in the last bus—known as "the drunks' special"—I stood on the moving disk between the two sections, which turned slightly on the curves. The floor of the long, tunnel-like vehicle rose, fell, and tilted this way and that; an empty beer bottle kept rolling under one of the seats and then out again. The two arms gripping the overhead wires not only conveyed the needed current but seemed also to save the bus and its passengers from sinking into the earth; following their example, I clutched the hanging straps above me with both hands.

It was a short ride; at that late hour, the bus went no farther than the cemetery. By then, I was the only passenger. I didn't get out until asked to, and then I took elaborate leave of the driver, becoming more verbose from step to step. "Good night, Mr. Chinaman," said the driver, and started round the circle on his way back to the city.

My housing development was still a long way off; for me, it couldn't be far enough. For a moment, the bus wires against the open sky veered off in the direction of a suburb in Japan. Shining in the lamplight, the gilt letters on the cemetery gate were an illegible script, or all the scripts in the world combined.

Something drew me westward, across the meadows to the canal. But at the moment that didn't seem to be my place. I stayed on the main road, which is bordered on the left by the cemetery wall, and as I walked I looked at the distant embankment—on my side of it the Canal Tavern, dark except for a single light in the upper story. The building, another symbol, looked to me like a lockhouse.

For a time I was alone on the road and imagined that Loner—like Loser, Hurler, and Spite—was a name. After a while, a man with hobnailed boots came along in the opposite direction and said in a malignant tone: "I know who you are, but you don't know who I am." As far as the end of the cemetery wall, I ran. The crematory amid the pines was lit up like some "sight" in the Old City. A yellow glove hung from a branch near the sidewalk. Above the road, the bus wires seemed to be woven into a steel net that wouldn't move before dawn.

The short stretch where the road rises—the Salzach, which has now been diverted eastward, used to flow here—gave me a chance to breathe deeply and I savored it. Though the former river terrace was not very high, the plain it led to—where the village of Gneis is situated— was definitely a plateau, and here the air was perceptibly colder. There was still snow in the fields, and where the earth showed through, it revealed a pattern resembling bird tracks. The mistletoe balls in the trees had white caps on. Icicles cut through the April foliage and reflected the night light with the clarity of glass. Birds chirped from tree to tree, as though eager to know whether their friends had lived through the storm.

I bent down and washed my eyes and temples in wet snow. I wished it would start snowing again. My lips and forehead thirsted for snow, as though I hadn't had my full share of winter yet.

In the suburb of Gneis, there was little light except for the streetlamps. An old old woman was standing at the window of a dark ground-floor room. The curtains were open and her face was close to the pane, but half concealed by her misted breath on the glass; no one would now have stood up to the look in her eyes.

Near the center of the village, the outlines of two children were painted on the roadway. The boy, who was a head taller, held his arm protectively around the girl. Both carried schoolbags. The sister was characterized by a pigtail, the brother by the prominence of his occiput. Under the layer of snow, the pair recurred several times in almost, but not quite, identical versions. The snow around them had melted, and the luminous paint glistened, though blackened from head to foot with tire marks.

I stood for a long time in the street, deep in contemplation of the schematic figures. Contemplation? In any event, there was nothing contemplative about the look I gave the driver of the oncoming car (who braked just in time), because he quickly closed the window he had already half opened and drove off without a word. Maybe he had only wanted to ask for directions—would the woman beside him otherwise have said: "Forget it, can't you see he's a stranger here himself?" And I called out after the car: "I'm only fit company for enemies now. Only my enemy is my friend." Since this enemy no longer existed, all that remained was an aimless "Wipe him out!" (But at the same time I thought: Lucky none of my pupils' parents was in that car.) Only then did I notice how many plays had been going on inside me, plays upon plays only a few hours before— and now not a single play was left. Or rather: I had run out of lines.

In the wooded section before the Colony, a mist arose. Only a few jutting branches could be made out clearly; trunks and treetops had almost disappeared. I dove into the mist as into a familiar element, one that suited me. The amount of space seemed infinite, and all for me. Suddenly on a tree trunk my shadow came to meet me.

I was almost disappointed when houses came into view; the gray of night was plenty of light for me. But in Oak Tree Colony I was—important to get this straight at such an hour—at home. The asphalt under my feet was home ground; this was in every sense *my* territory. Hadn't I once wanted to shout at a noisy group of foreigners in the Old City: "Quiet—this is Austria!"? My country: an enamel sign in a provincial railroad station showed a pointing hand, with the words: "To the well." My country, indeed. A man's own country meant refuge, he could defend himself.

"But would you also defend this country of yours?" "Perhaps not the parliament building" would be my answer to such a question, "but this barn and that vintner's hut, definitely." For I can say of myself: "I am sick with my country."

Now in the dense mist of the plain there was nothing but the Colony; no mountains, no sky; the desolation was almost complete. Some of the new houses were still unoccupied, and here and there the streets still smelled of fresh paint. The curtains of the foreign workers' houses were of various dark colors, and even on the fully laden clotheslines there was seldom anything white to be seen. A barn glowed with inner light, shadows of animal bodies and human heads moved about and intermingled, as though a mare or a cow were being delivered. By the football field, a landfill far out on the heath, the dark tavern was being guarded by a dog named Nadir du Mistral with glass eyes and ears that resembled horns. A short, fierce, peacock-like screech issued from the Home for Retarded Children; a fluorescent light flickered; the windows were open at the top and the blinds hung down at a slant. A car had just driven into the garage; the top was covered with snow mixed with greenery; the driver, his hands on the wheel, was listening to the news on the radio; the only light in the villa that went with the garage was in the aquarium, where ornamental fish slowly swam back and forth.

I sat down by the canal, on a bench next to the phone booth, facing the apartment house where I lived. From time to time, the wind whistled through a solitary spruce by the water. I shut my eyes. Behind me, the Alm, almost silent over the rest of its course, roared like rapids— at this point, it drops steeply. Had I slept? When I opened my eyes, there was the half-moon with the face of a decrepit old man; a spruce branch was waving like a bird's plume in front of it. In the moment of my awakening, the whole tree darkened and became my shadow.

I went into the house and without turning the light on anywhere, either at the entrance or in my apartment, went straight to bed. I lay with my eyes shut and began to feel warm. The mountain that goes by my name appeared to me. (It's known to me only from a picture.) Mount Loser stood detached under a spacious sky, as though in a sphere of its own; and yet it seemed only a few steps away. From a rounded hilltop, which formed the pedestal, rose the naked cliffs of its gigantic upper story. Its flat roof was covered by a deep layer of snow, overarched by transparent gray air. The snow lay in wavelike dunes, and on the side of the mountain a white fountain surged into the gray air—a sign that a storm was raging up there. It must have been a severe storm, because the snow cloud was long and almost horizontal; indeed, it had a slight upward tilt. At the same time, the scene, beheld from a distance, seemed perfectly still; even the white of the fountain was motionless. In the sheer wall below it, there were dark spots, almost like gates or niches. Open, O gate in the rock. Take palpable form, O Aeolian Mount Loser.

Yet no peace came. Something was missing, something without which any appeal to any object whatsoever was premature. And premature meant pointless. The object ceased to be a thing of this world. "Something is missing" meant: there was room within me, but it remained empty. I did not expect the missing thing, I couldn't—I had no reason to expect it. There was simply an unfilled space within me—and its emptiness was sorrow.

"But what is this thing that is not to be expected? The rustling of a tree that becomes a voice? A fountain rising from a cliff? A burning bush? Why not admit for once that what you lack is love!"

At this point, I finally lost my temper. "What kind of love are you people driving at? Love between the sexes? Love for another person? Love of nature? Love for what one has created? I, in any case, am homesick just now for a body, and not for its sex, but for beloved shoulders, a beloved cheek, a beloved glance, a beloved presence. Love? Incapacity for love? Lover's sorrow? The sorrow is present only now that I am without love. You have only invented 'incapacity' as a pretext for your loveless argument. And when love sets in, I won't have to appeal to the distant mountain anymore; of its own accord, it will move into our sphere, a salt dome, confirmation of thy, my presence. With the onset of love, I shall be safe. Or it will not have been love."

The Viewer Seeks a Witness

n the days that followed, I didn't leave the house. Most of the time I lay prone on my bed, my head in the crook of my arm. This arm was a kind of bulwark, behind which I felt sheltered. Now and then I'd pick up a daddy longlegs and let it run about in the palm of my hand, which tickled pleasantly. Occasionally I'd lie on my back, looking at the wall, where a flashlight and a shoehorn were hanging on a hook.

Outside the window, two thick ropes hung down; the housefront was being renovated and they served to pull a basket filled with mortar up and to lower one that had been emptied. In the dawning light, the ropes seemed strikingly massive and dark. At night, they made themselves noticed now and then by slapping against the windowpanes. In the moonlight, they glistened like glass; the melting snow had run over them during the day and then frozen.

The phone rang fairly often; but it was only someone who had dialed a wrong number—as if Salzburg were the city not only of disorderly pedestrians but also of disorderly telephoners. Finally, after calls for the "parish office," for a man called Siegfried, for the "customs office for overseas shipments" and Part-Time, Inc., I shouted into the phone: "Shut up!" After that, I stopped answering.

In the morning, my mail fell through the door slot: advertisements, and one solitary letter, consisting of a printed form titled "News Flash," with a check mark in the margin.

During the day, the sounds from the supermarket provided distraction. When it was closed for lunch hour,

I waited almost impatiently for the beep of the cash registers to resume.

Of course, all this could be told in a different way. When I looked in the mirror, there were no eyes. I felt as if I had no body left; that is, I no longer had any share in the light and wind, in the cold or heat; and this was a privation. As I lay there without dignity, I was a painful husk; a husk with nothing inside. In the absence of a viewer, there was nothing left to view. Once, in the dusk, I confused the gigantic Untersberg with a wooded knoll. Another time, I saw a cliff as a flashing guillotine. A volcano had erupted in the Staufen; great gray-violet clouds of smoke drifted from its pyramidal summit; and when again I looked westward, the whole mountain had collapsed into a rubble heap only half its height. (In reality, the main peak was hidden by rain clouds, so only the much smaller front peak could be seen.) And what did "west" mean? The cardinal points had become meaningless, as they do for one cast adrift on the open sea; in the place of direction, confusion reigned. When once I made an attempt to dress, I missed all the openings and stood there like a twisted malefactor (funny, I have to admit). I heard sounds as when the Föhn is blowing; they seemed to come not from my field of vision but from around the corner, so to speak, from behind my back, taking me unawares, without the corresponding visual images. The everyday cries of the jackdaws rang out like bursts of gunfire; I suddenly heard the clip-clop of a horse's hoofs as though a stopped clock had started (it would stop again in an instant); cocks crowed as though sounding the alarm, or taps. And whenever the bus wires struck together in the woods out-side, a crashing and a crackling were heard as when a big building is on fire.

Often there was something to laugh about: once, some horses actually turned up at the bus terminus, hitched to cabs that seemed to have come to this wilderness by mistake. Inside them sat exotic tourists, aiming their cameras without conviction at the Colony. But I didn't laugh.

Yet I didn't think there was anything wrong with me. In fact, I felt a strange satisfaction at "exposing" my-self, just as there can be a certain satisfaction in exposing oneself to total darkness or a glacial wind—in laying oneself open to the worst sort of adversity. Satisfaction? No, pleasure. Pleasure? No, determination. Determina-tion? No, acquiescence in the conditions of existence.

In all those days, I never once felt anything akin to guilt. What I felt was something worse. I had thrust a long knitting needle so accurately into someone's heart that there was not so much as a cut to be seen in the outer skin, and everybody was congratulating me over it. But I saw myself from then on as living in—the word cannot be avoided—perdition. (And there were no hands with which to cover the face of him who had seen it; if any-one had shouted "Hands up!" I'd have left them dang-ling at my side, and not out of contempt for death.) When people come home from work in the evening, don't they sometimes sigh while settling into a chair: "How good it feels to finally be able to sit down!" But, with me, sitting had the opposite effect. Nothing made me feel good. Only perhaps I should avoid the word "perdition" and say instead: "The bouncing bird, the cat washing itself, were lacking in the center of my field of vision." In the center there was nothing, neither a playing dog nor a swaying daddy longlegs (or, if there was, it fled instantly). Or there was something in the center, but nothing pleasant. Once a freshly shot pair of chamois were hanging in the open garage of a villa, still dripping blood, hanging by their horns from two hooks, face to face. Even a bird and a cat appeared, but they were corpses drifting in the canal. Or the center was a place of staggering illusions: the light-colored logs lying crosswise at the end of the meadow looked like a dead ox; a seesawing brimstone butterfly appeared to me repeatedly as a scrap of yellowish paper. Or the center was a place of disillusionment; when I looked for it, it was hidden by billboards or by exotic shrubs with their unreal colors. Or the center itself was falsified: the house next door, raised by an artificially filled-in terrace, had a bell tower on the ridge of its roof in the manner of old farmhouses—but the area below the terrace seemed eroded, the shrine over the door of the house meant only: "You are not welcome here"—and the little bell tower, taken as a center, framed a mere hole: because the bell belonging to it, or the clapper, or the bellpull, was missing. By day, this hole often suggested a whirl of clotted milk, and by night, at best, an artificial satellite broadcasting the latest news of wars and disasters. The worst of these falsifications in those days were the so-called natural centers, occupied by the church towers, at least one of which "naturally" catches the eye at every turn of the head. Not only did these steeples, whether bulbiform,

conical, or cylindrical, strike me as pretentious; I also
regarded them as petrified delusions, making a mockery of our—all men's—forlornness. Nobody needed
them, but they set themselves up as friends in need. Even
in misery, didn't the horizon sometimes send us light and
air, which wanted to be let in and seen? And these
steeples cut off the view.

What I missed this particular Holy Week was the
usual ringing of the bells. I hungered for it. It seemed
inconceivable to me that a thinker some decades ago
should have praised the big cities of the Communist
world on the ground that the "deadly sad Western ringing of bells had been done away with." The bells were
silent. I was not content with the whistling of the wind.
Nor with the roaring of the canal down at the rapids.
Nor with the monotonously musical electrical purring
of the approaching buses. I was reminded of a passage
in a writer of the last century who praised the Roman
poet Lucretius, saying that for him the "black pit was
infinity itself," and that his era, extending from Cicero
to Marcus Aurelius, represented a moment unique in
history, "when the gods were dead and Christ had not
yet been born, when man alone existed." During the
days when the bells were silent and the wind whistled
and the buses purred, or so at least it seemed to me later
on, I relived that era.

Yet my experience was rather different from that of
the poet Lucretius, allegedly so heroic in his godless-
ness. It seemed to me as obvious as it was unthinkable
that I alone, a human being with death as his goal, existed. Something was lacking, but not Christ and not the

gods, and not the immortal soul, but something physical:
a sensory organ, the crucial one, without which the
whistling of the wind and the purring of the buses remain incomplete.

Often in the past, glancing at a distant mountain ridge,
I had seen a procession of climbers without beginning
or end, and thought in spite of myself of the famous trek
to the gold fields; and in this procession, I, the viewer,
was a dark, heavily laden figure among others. However
often I looked, that gently rising line, broken by the
tops of spruce trees, was uninhabited, orphaned. The
lines up and down the pass yielded no human pyramid.
How can I give a more accurate picture of the sense that
I lacked? Perhaps only Greek has a verb expressing that
fusion of perception and imagination (which is essen-
tial). On the surface, this verb means only "to notice";
but it carries overtones of "white," "bright," "radiance,"
"glitter," "shimmer." Within me there was an outright
longing for this radiance, which is more than any sort
of viewing. I shall always long for that kind of seeing,
which in Greek is called *leukein*.

While I waited for the big bells to come back, I conceived an incredible hatred of animals—not so much
of birds as of all four- or more-legged animals. The
birds with their soaring flight seemed to draw invisible
communication lines through the air. But I despised all
earthbound animals because, as far as I could see, they
gave no thought to any kind of resurrection. They merely
huddled, crept, crawled, scurried about, lurked, rutted,
or dozed. I almost sympathized with the cruelty of children who kill cats and pull the legs off daddy longlegs.

Yet at the same time it seemed to me that I was reliving the origin of certain Easter rites—when, for instance, I glimpsed the fresh, fleshy white of a horseradish root, dug from deep in the ground; taken together with the lumps of earth clinging to it, that white struck me as a plausible color for life.

All through the weekend I lay stretched out on my bed, incapable of the slightest movement, clenching my teeth and fists, if you can call that lying. Early in the morning, a woman down in the street, who evidently worked in a pastry shop, said: "We're having a heavy run on Easter eggs." At noon, the shutters of the supermarket were pulled down for three days. For a long while, in the afternoon, a little bird fluttered up and down outside my window.

With a package tour from somewhere, I landed on the airfield of the moon. From the lobby of the air terminal building, a stairway led down to a restaurant that was jam-packed with Chinese. It was a sinister den, dimly lit and low-ceilinged. In the middle there was a platform—this was the place of slaughter. Naked men with long, curved, two-handed swords flung themselves on other naked but unarmed men. There was no struggle. Nor did the unarmed men run away. They buckled like apes overtaken by a pursuing lion, bared their teeth, and hissed (or rather squeaked) their last cries of terror at the butchers. The soles of the victims' feet seemed also to buckle and formed high, loudly creaking arches on the platform. A moment later, the whole body was gone. Not only had it been cut into little pieces, but almost simultaneously it had been devoured by the people in the room below. What an instant before had been part of a gesticulating human being was now a chunk of meat vanishing into someone's gullet. The mouths with these unceasingly active gullets marked, as it were, the innermost core of the Chinese quarter, which at one time had been the hub of all world happening. The slaughter would never end. Time and again, new loads of arms and shoulders were brought in, and in the place of these arms and shoulders there would once again be nothing. We travelers were separated by ropes from the place of slaughter. Bags in hand, we quickly left the airport. The moon was not our final destination; we now went to an elevator at the edge of the airfield, which was to take us back to earth. On the way, we walked under the open sky. Tall acacias rustled in a pale light such as foreshadows a cloudburst. It was not, as one might have expected, easy to walk in the lunar atmosphere—we didn't hover. From step to step, our limbs grew heavier. I had no difficulty breathing, but felt that I soon would have. It was still a long way to the elevator stop, a windowless, sheet-metal shack, which was ringed by people waiting with suitcases. The only hope was to wake up. But I couldn't manage to.

At length, the bundle on the bed opened its eyes and sat up. There was a color in the room. It came from the hibiscus plant growing in a large flowerpot next to the wall; a single blossom had opened, carmine against a purple, almost black ground. The pale pink pistil in the middle gleamed like the glass core of a lightbulb, and at the tip were the erect orange-yellow stamens. The flower was within reaching distance, and I held out my hand toward it. I had tried to feel it the day before, but all sense of touch had gone out of my fingers, and I had thought that the still-unfolding flower, as so often with hibiscus flowers, had already shriveled. Now I held a living weight, which cooled my hand and regulated my pulse.

What in the morning had been adulterated by the stench of tomcats now resolved itself into the fragrance of the apples spread out on the shelf. It must have been late afternoon, for the open door of the west room no longer admitted sunshine, but only a deep-yellow glow, in which the hibiscus plant cast on the wall a cloudy shape and within it a few clearly delineated stem shadows. "Late afternoon" reminds me that my son once said it was depressing to keep reading in stories: "At dusk"—it would be better, he thought, to say: "In the late afternoon." "They arrived in the late afternoon."

I stood up and looked around; I had never seen a more beautiful room. I bent over the hibiscus blossom. A daddy longlegs was groping its way over the wall, and I addressed it roughly as follows: "Oh. So that's it. Aha. Hmm. Very well. Good. Why not?"

I took a long shower. Under the warm water, my body gradually grew out of itself. Stationary leg and free-moving leg took form. I took deep swallows of the liquid that would have choked me a few hours before.

In the kitchen, I ate a whole package of zwieback and recalled a saying I had often heard as a child: "Dizziness takes the appetite away." I had been dizzy for days and now I was hungry. I ate an apple and knew at the first bite that I would go on eating.

Seated at my desk, I put my manuscript, "Thresholds of the Roman Villa," into an envelope, addressed it, and affixed stamps. Only a short while before, I would have looked on without lifting a finger as every page of it burned or flew out the window. I read a letter from the school principal, who had once been my teacher and later became my friend. In it, he said I was expected back after Easter vacation, that the students had been asking for me, that the undersigned missed me—and not just in his official capacity. A postscript followed: "Please don't forget that you're a teacher. Even if your manner isn't right, you are nevertheless an effective teacher, precisely because you are not entirely of the profession. What enables you to teach is your slight embarrassment, coupled with your total immersion in your subject. There are more than enough competent teachers. But students get the feel of a subject only from those who are at times visibly embarrassed at being teachers, from stutterers and thread-losers. Only such a one remains fixed in the student's memory as 'my teacher.' *Quin age.* Let us then be up and doing!"

The reader of the letter sat down and wept; not over the praise, but over the salutation, "Dear Andreas," for it seemed to me that for years no one had called me by my first name.

Still seated, I opened the window. The west wind grazed my neck and temples. In inhaling, I was taken with a violent coughing fit; all those days, I hadn't once breathed deeply. A horse snorted beside me; that horse was me, as if my nostrils had suddenly grown.

The word "vision" has gone out of fashion. But a vision is just what I had then. I saw the ship of my life, caught in pack ice and already half under water, suddenly rise to the surface and go dancing away. Though the water might be no more than a rivulet and my ship a scrap of paper, perplexity was instantly transformed into a cheerfulness which was anything but caprice and which for the first time could be relied on.

At the same time, though, I realized that the murderous stone I had thrown a few days past marked the beginning of my own death. Since then, there had been something deadly in me, something that could be played down—as I was doing now—but not eradicated. I was no longer in a state of suspense—and my present light-headedness had grief as its companion. To play down meant power. "Power" meant: "I have time."

I sat down at my desk, picked up a pencil, and wrote in the flyleaf of Virgil's *Georgics*: "Not an unfortunate accident, but destiny. Take accident as destiny. Not mine, but everyone's. Destiny as man's lot. Not his human lot, but his share. Distinguish two sorts of human destiny: lot and share. Man's lot: as everyone knows, to die. His share? All I know is that if I haven't had my share, I shall die without having fulfilled my destiny. My share is up to me; to obtain it, that is, I must challenge it. From disaster to destiny. Through destiny to self-awareness. I am determined and self-determined.

Surrender? Yes, but not to any judge. No, I will not 'surrender,' I will seek out a witness. What for? To ask for advice. Who will be my witness? And time and again 'the threshold'; lest you pass it by, slow down to a child's pace. No, don't slow down; restrain yourself. —Sunflower in the mist. —The epithet for hibiscus in Virgil: slender."

A pyramid of wood for the Easter bonfire, heaped up at the point where the road passes into the meadow, was illumined by the last light of day. I went from window to window, this way and that, through the whole apartment. Now and then, on the slopes, a trial cannon shot rang out. A freshly washed bus was waiting at the terminus; with its two long, thick arms, it looked like a great stag. For a moment, the portholes of a plane taking off became transparent, revealing the bright blue sky behind them; for a long while, flocks of black crows followed its sooty trail, just as gulls follow the wake of a ship. Below, a child popped paper bags while walking in the street—his version of an Easter salute; while a teenager ran back and forth in an orchard, snapping a whip, which at every crack sent little clouds of smoke rising between the treetops.

This time, a different couple were sitting on the bridge railing: an elderly man in a double-breasted suit with a pocket handkerchief, tie, and white shirt, holding a younger woman close, murmuring and whispering as he rubbed his head against hers, and occasionally prodding her with his forehead; if they should fall into the canal, I thought, the water would hiss as if something red-hot had been dropped in.

Otherwise, the streets were deserted. But, undoubtedly, crowds were pouring into the churches for the Feast of the Resurrection. The mountains looked blue; then gray; then black. The rows of light at the airfield suggested a fiery cross, traversed by a constantly renewed arrow. The border station on the horizon gleamed like a factory decked out for a holiday.

Love welled up in me for this city in the plain. Its cityness. Substance of joy. The earth awakened within me, with a white Mayan city on the chalk cliffs of Yucatán, and with Heraclitus, warming himself by his stove and calling out to visitors: "Come in. Here, too, there are gods." I wanted to throw myself on the ground, but not alone. At that moment, a single word sufficed: "Here!"

At length, the cathedral bells rang out in the distance. There the ritual of transubstantiation was being enacted: bread into "body," wine into "blood." The bell sounded twice, both times very briefly. It was as though a heart that had stopped beating began to beat again. A horse raised its head and showed its great eye with its light-colored, bristling lashes. The beaks of the gulls were at their sharpest and most hooked.

Little by little, the bells began to ring throughout the city area. I distinguished the bells of Elsbethen, of Aigen, of Persch, of Gnigl, of Sankt Andrä, of Maria Plain, of Bergheim, of Freilassing (across the border), of Bayrischgmain, of Grossgmain (back on this side), of Liefering, of Wals, of Gois, of Taxham, of Grödig, of Anif, of Morzg, of Gneis; the bells of the Meadow Church, of the Moos Church, of the Old People's Home

Church, of the Dormitory Church, of the Poorhouse
Church.

During the night, there was a violent knocking on the
water pipes. The hibiscus blossom rolled up and fell off
its stem, with a very soft sound. A warm wind blew
through the wide-open room. There was a smell of wood
smoke. Even before the first bus arrived, I heard a
twanging in the wires like a catapult in action, followed
by a crash, as between two hockey sticks. Up until then,
it had been so quiet that the waterfalls in the mountains
could be heard. Later on, a strange melody sounded
from end to end of the plain. In my half-sleep—which
was more like a special kind of waking—separate sounds
answered one another and thus became music. A train
whistle was followed by the rumble of a steel grating
under rolling wheels. The rumbling was taken up by a
barking dog. The dog's barking took on the tone of the
wind in the trees, which in turn blended into the en-
veloping sound of a short rainfall. Actually, it was not
so much a melody as a leitmotif prolonged indefinitely.
Every new sound took it up and intensified it. Every object that emitted a sound swelled, as it were, in my
imagination and vibrated, converted into a musical instrument. Plucked instruments, percussion and wind
instruments rang out, interspersed with an infrequent but
precisely timed violin tone, as though from a mountain
lake freezing over. The sound of the rain was rhythmed
by a vibraphone-like ringing far below the road, rising
from the round openings of the manhole cover. I had
once taken the children to see a film in which terrestrial

and extraterrestrial beings conversed by means of such a persistently repeated motif. Had extraterrestrial beings landed now, and was this sound their signal? No, this was an earthly sound, an earthly creature lay dreaming, and his breathing through a single orifice fed the earthly orchestra. Dreaming? I had never felt so wide-awake. A more delightful wake-up music was unthinkable.

I arose with the first light and washed the windows and floors of both my rooms. Outside, the bog appeared with its earth colors—green, brown, ocher, and black. It was blanketed in haze, purple in the dawning light. The great flank of the Staufen emerged from the western horizon, shimmering white like a strange star. "Beloved colors! It is by contemplating you that we live."

I dressed after laying garment after garment over my arm like my own valet: blue-and-white-striped shirt, silk tie, double-breasted summer suit, black low-cut leather shoes, long, light-gray "dustcoat"; and into my breast pocket I slipped the hibiscus blossom, which had shrunk to a reddish cigar. I went to the mirror, looked for a long while into my eyes, and for once found myself beautiful. I filed my nails to a perfect roundness. With a single unbroken movement, I put my hat on. I leafed through my paper money, rolled it up, and thrust it into my trouser pocket. I left my apartment without locking the door.

On the street, an old crone, her face and neck a network of wrinkles forming innumerable tiny hexagons, approached and said: "Here comes Mr. Springtime." The cracks in the asphalt at the edge of the street also formed a hexagonal pattern. A young man in uniform, wearing pointed shoes and carrying a suitcase, crossed the canal bridge. As the sun rose, a dog ran down a path through the meadow, swaying from side to side against the light like a covered wagon in the Wild West. And I did indeed bear westward, though from time to time I veered off to the north and south; or just stood there for a while. Now and then, I walked backward and then I had the eastern sun in my face. The sun didn't disperse the ground haze but gave it a bright color. Later, it took on a lasting lilac hue, against which the branches of the trees looked intensely black.

On the Untersberg, there was snow only above the tree line; the plateau at the top was mottled with it. The whole mountain was sharply outlined; every gully and every crag stood out distinctly; only the hollow below the summit seemed a caldron of clouds, sending out spiral after spiral of mist. One of these took the shape of a giant eagle and went flying over the plain, hunting with talons outstretched and an eye of azure blue.

In crossing the thinly settled area, I met no one. Only once I saw someone on another path, and we greeted each other with upraised hats. On my way, I stopped into the Moos church, where services were in progress. Only a few people were there, at a certain point in the Mass, they gave one another their hands. Each of those present was expected to make a holiday wish. A woman with a polka-dotted head scarf said: "May Austria never die." A young man said aloud: "May we become holy." Two children looked at each other and grinned.

I left right after the blessing and went my way. The

bog was rather bumpy in spots where peat had formerly been dug and which were now overgrown with grass. Here and there a patch of fallow land had been fenced off to form a community garden; from a gate that put one in mind of a ranch, a long, wide gravel path led to wooden cottages in the background.

The airport control tower, the tallest building on the whole plain, looked like an armless robot in the distance. I started toward it on a railroad track that came from the loading platform of a brewery. The warehouse was a long, yellow building with only blind windows in front. The sun shone on the great empty triangle and was reflected back. Momentarily overlapping, the shadows of two butterflies moved about on one of the blind windows as on a dance floor; the empty triangular space around them was a shimmering symbol of freedom. The railroad tracks in the meadow grass gave off a dazzling light. The ties forced me to take short steps like an old man; afterward, on the road, away from the tracks, I continued to move in their rhythm. A lone locomotive had once traversed this meadow, covered from roof to running board with homeward-bound workers.

The road enters a long tunnel which passes under the airport. Just before the tunnel, there is an athletic field, screened from view by a dense crowd, over which for a moment a white ball appeared. On a recurrent billboard, a blond woman posing in violet lingerie informed all comers: "These curves are for loving." The highway was heavily traveled. Cars emerged from the tunnel with their headlights on; some turned them off at once, some a little later, some not at all. ("That's the way we are.") One car still had skis on top; the next, flowers; the third was already carrying a boat. A woman, perceptible only as a tapering hand on the wheel, held a long, skin-colored cigarette between her fingers and left behind her the image of a praying mantis. Utterly soundless in comparison to the crashing and honking on the ground, an enormous flying object, a commercial plane coming in for a landing, entered the air space above the endless column of vehicles. For a moment, it seemed motionless; only when it put down on the runway did it fill the countryside with its howling.

In the tunnel, the noise of the cars swelled to a roar and a blast, which passed through the portholes in the concrete wall and spread to the parallel foot and bicycle paths. A chain of fluorescent lights made the tunnel into a seemingly endless sequence of light and dark chambers, where pedestrians were by turns luminescent and invisible. The walls were covered with graffiti. The firstcomers had spread out freely, the rest had to squeeze in: *Young man seeks young woman, view to sexual intercourse; Zion, devil's-bread tree; Mother, your son is still walking under the sky; Kondwiramur.* Two soldiers in caps and laced shoes saluted me in passing and called out: "Morning, Colonel. At your service." Then came an unshaven man on a bicycle, who just said: "Hey, you." (I, in turn, said to a woman who was running: "What's the hurry?") There was a cool, fresh smell in the tunnel. At the other end, it opened out to the west wind. The asphalt, pockmarked from stiletto heels and hobnails, looked, if you kept your eyes on it, like a dusty country road, spotted with raindrops.

Leaves blown in from outside showed that the tunnel was nearing its end. The section of landscape which came into view at the exit seemed suffused with a sort of transcontinental light. Here the Staufen is seen from a new angle; the accustomed pyramidal top breaks down into three broad humps, which draw the eye into the distance, and the gas stations, the warehouses, and the hangar begin to look like some sort of overseas settlement—in Tierra del Fuego or Montana.

The airport is correspondingly small, as if it were not part of the city but some sort of colonial branch office. The birches outside the terminal building were snow-white, and the luminous green of the young shoots of a larch tree seemed to fill the tree with tiny exotic birds. The stone rocket in the forecourt was replicated in the grass plot below it by a similarly shaped unopened crocus, whose dark violet emerged, ready for takeoff, from its silver-gray involucre.

Now it was midday and warm. Even the short wings of the ubiquitous sparrows sparkled in the sunlight whenever they flew up out of the hedges. From the fields adjoining the airport came waves of manure smell, and cows and pigs bellowed in the former Roman settlement of Loig, a little farther on. The straight line to the horizon drawn by the yellow laburnum bushes on either side of the highway was accentuated by the yellow of a gas station. As usual, I misread a "long-term parking" sign as "long-term farting."

The air terminal building has two stories, surmounted by an observation deck. The second floor is occupied by a restaurant and a so-called hotel. This hotel consists of a short corridor with a few rooms on either side, so narrow that the two beds in it have to be placed end-to-end. In most of the rooms, the windows look out on the nearby control tower and the runways. Except in summer, the hotel is almost always empty; occasionally, a group will arrange for a banquet in the restaurant and book rooms in the hotel as well. There are no night flights.

The reception desk, behind a glass door that is always open, was, as usual, untended. I got the key from a waiter, whom I found in the terrace café. All the rooms were vacant, he informed me, and they were all the same. I wrote two names in the register: Andreas Loser and Tilia Levis. At least the waiter regarded the latter as a name, for he asked me: "Isn't that an actress?" He had a bushy black mustache and said, without waiting for my answer: "Or an aviator? Or a foreigner? I'm from Kurdistan."

It was cold and dark in the room; under the curtain rods and in the shower stall, the hum of fluorescent light. But when the window was open, warm spring air and quiet sunlight filled the room. The airfield didn't seem to function at midday; there was only a helicopter flying back and forth, close to the ground as though looking for something, like a rescue craft over the ocean. Up in the glassed-in control tower, a man was sitting at the radar screen; he had his headphones on and he was reading the paper.

In the restaurant, I chose a table by the window, with a view of the western villages and mountains. In the middle of a fenced-in grass plot, a feathery brown spruce tree glimmered beside a chapel-blue fire hydrant. I ate light-colored lamb and drank burgundy, which in the bottle was as black as belladonna and in the glass barberry red—they brought out the colors of the landscape.

I spent the afternoon in the village of Loig, at the excavation site (which had been partly filled in). In the pits that were still open, children were looking for mosaic stones that might have been overlooked, and an elderly gentleman with chunks of clay clinging to the soles of his shoes—he had no doubt walked across the fields—was sketching the ancient water conduits in a notebook. A fruit tree, all pink-and-white blossoms, stood by itself in a muddy enclosure; a plump hen and a titmouse were perched on two branches, one above the other—living proof that such diversity of forms and species cannot be mere chance.

Later on, in the air terminal building, where the sun had begun to turn orange and the unoccupied ticket windows seemed extraordinarily massive, an early passenger or greeter was sitting alone in the waiting room, which suggested a bus terminal more than an airport. Later the room filled up. The people standing there had long shadows. The windows were manned, the baggage conveyor belts running. And in the Rent-a-Car stalls—those of one company red, of the other yellow—the mascaraed lashes, the bleached hair, and the hands with lacquered fingernails resumed their places. A uniformed guard with a submachine gun crossed the room, his head tilted slightly back, his eyes half closed, as pale and stiff as a corpse.

Something drew me to all these people, even though

the air inside was close and smelled like fermented stale bread.

The sun went down. In the parking lot, which had been deserted all afternoon, long lines of cabs were now waiting with their roof lights on. A movement ran through the leafy plants that twine through the whole lobby, as though in accompaniment to the song pouring from the transistor radio that a young fellow in the shell chair beside me was holding up to his ear. A dog barked and the glassed-in lobby transformed the sound into the wailing of a pinball machine. The plane that was just landing would fly on immediately to another country. It was the end of the holiday; an unusually large number of passengers got out or pressed toward the entrance on the other side. Newly arrived passengers, waiting for their luggage, were unrecognizable shadows behind a frosted-glass door, while friends and relatives crowded around a narrow opening to wave or to signal in some other way. A traveler emerged from the automatic double doors, walked over to one of the Rent-a-Car stalls, where the girl in charge, leaning over the counter like a seller of lottery tickets, held out a finger with car keys on it; he grabbed them in his mouth and at the same time snapped at her finger, which the girl did not pull back but thrust in a little deeper. While the man rushed out to his car, the girl unfolded a piece of paper he had tossed to her, and slipped it under the telephone.

I sat bolt-upright, my legs close together and my hands on my knees. Outside, over the road to the city, a strange new signal shone amid the usual traffic lights, billboards, and cranes: the rising, fiery-red full moon. Inside, between the wings of the door, a young woman appeared. Half hidden by the people in front of her and darkened by those behind her, she was visible as a line from neck to hip. I stood up and took off my hat. In disengaging herself from the crowd, the woman stumbled and described a semicircle. Then, standing to one side, she turned away from the exit, as though wishing in that way to attract someone's attention.

No one came. The last cab drove away. The plane took off. As it rose into the air, the din it had just made in speeding over the runway bounced back from the Untersberg. The whole rocky mass was still rumbling and roaring, while the plane was already far in the distance, no bigger than a dragonfly. Had the woman's back, along with the triangle of her scarf, come closer in the meantime, or had they receded? The lobby was almost empty when at last she turned around. Her face revealed a thoughtful beauty; of all beauties, the most thoughtful.

First, she looked out at the fields through the plate-glass front; then at the hat in my hand, as though this were a prearranged sign of recognition; and, last, into my eyes. It was a two-way glance that nothing could cancel out, though after it we blinked into empty space as if something terrifying had happened. She said something in an indeterminate accent, but the accent may have been only momentary. I went over to her and took her in my arms. I was overwhelmed by the one word that was spoken between us: *"Du."*

We went slowly up to the second floor; or possibly we ran. I took the key from the untended reception desk. The short corridor seemed to have widened into a suite of rooms. The spotlights in the ceiling cast a procession of circles on the carpet. There was no sound but the soft whirring of the lamps.

She jostled me with her hip, intentionally or perhaps not. She laughed at the room, but the look in my eyes made her grave. She stumbled, or pretended to stumble, across the threshold, which was only a strip of grooved hard rubber.

Seen in the slanted windowpanes of the control tower, the headlights of the cars driving straight on the road below were moving in curves. On the abandoned tables of the workers' cafeteria stood glass sugar bowls, their lids all casting identical round shadows on the white crystals underneath. In a dark room to one side, an electric iron and a baby's bottle were discernible on the windowsill.

Through the dark hotel room, whose only light came from the airfield—a multicolored dotted pattern on the walls—ran a shudder, followed by stillness. Does an individual, doubled up in dying, circling around himself, not sometimes feign to be two hostile beings locked in a life-and-death struggle? Here, for once, the reverse was true: two beings quietly side by side, not dying. Far enough apart to bring them close. Someone asked: "Do you remember?" as though there were a memory in common. Someone said: "Then 'weakness' is another word for 'being in the right.' " No one said: "Save me"; at the very most, "Help me."

The room was cramped, yet the two bodies made space for themselves. We fitted nicely into one of the beds, at the foot of which lay a white, towel-size mat. Looking for her in the dark, I sensed her presence all the more deeply. No, no need to look for her. She was there. Moved to the core by her body's being there, I hesitated —and by my hesitation she knew me. Yes, it was the woman who recognized the man; and it was she who with a resolute, majestic gesture united with him.

In passion, our bodies did not diverge but remained together. They consummated the act, which was not a frenzied struggle but a mighty game, the "game of games." In that night of love, another time reckoning and another sense of place took over. Now it's raining (the wet concrete runway is a quiet lake). Now the full moon is shining on a little gondola-shaped cloud with two lovers in it. Now the shower of sparks from the inter-secting bus wires is in your body. Now your shoulder is your face again. Now the eastern sky is a Spanish-lilac color. Now for a moment the woman's speaking becomes a singing. She means nothing by it; she is only singing her beauty.

Dreams came. I stepped out of the story, walked down a sloping meadow by night; the brook at the foot of it shimmered in the morning sun; there were human silhouettes on the bank. Was it another dream when, head tilted back, I looked into a woman's womb as into the inner recesses of a cupola tapering from turn to turn? When I wanted to convince myself, the eyes of a beautiful stranger rested on me. It must have been a dream in any case that, one with each other, we became a native of the world's center.

The strange face with the closed eyelids and lips made me think of a primeval stone figure, expressing—it is uncertain which—bliss, mischief, or danger; in the next moment, it might smile at me or spit at me or both at once. Instead, it opened its eyes and looked at me; and a woman's voice—anonymous no longer—said: "I must leave you now. It's late."

Outside, a procession of small cars with blinking lights on top drove along the runway. During the night, the moon had waned a little. A baggage truck rattled; a gate opened in the parking area. Smoke rose from the farmhouse at the end of the runway; in the courtyard, a slowly striding male figure on his way to the barn.

When I asked her when I would be seeing her again, she replied: "Once upon a time there were." Did that mean that wishes were in order? "Not wishes, but questions." So I asked her how she saw me. I was in need of being described a little. "Give me a portrait of myself. It can be false if you like."

Then she replied: "You don't seem to be wholly present; you breathe discontent. You're kind of run-down. I desire you but I don't trust you. You have something on your conscience; not theft, or you'd be on the run. It's plain that you are outside ordinary law, and it makes you suffer in a way. I don't trust you, and I do. You are like the man in the doorway. Though very ill, he went to see a good friend. In leaving, he stopped at length in the doorway and tried to smile; his tensed eyes became slits, framed in their sockets as by sharply ground lenses. 'Goodbye, my suffering Chinaman,' said his friend."

"Did they ever see each other again?"

The portraitist said nothing more. Already in the doorway, her only reply was an immensely friendly laugh. I shut my eyes and heard a sort of answer after all: "In the end, the friend said to the friend, 'At last a Chinese—at last a Chinese face among so many native faces.' "

That morning, I cut across the fields and visited my mother in Wals. She lives in an old people's home on the large, almost always deserted village square. We sat together in the garden, on a wooden bench under a pear tree with pink-and-white blossoms.

At first she mistook me for the postman, and later she addressed me by various other names. From time to time she recognized me, and then she giggled, keeping her mouth closed to hide the stumps of her teeth. Her eyes were very bright, her face as small as a child's, her head no bigger than a headhunter's shrunken trophy. She was eating an Easter egg, more scraping than biting, and the painted shells fell into her lap; she gulped the whole yolk down at once. She studied me at length and then said: "Aren't these cruel times we're living in? Even before you went away to the army, I was always sorry for you." She asked me how my "business," as she called it, was getting along. "You and your business," a traditional turn of phrase, which was not meant to be disparaging, but betokened a sort of respectful awe. And then another strange word fell: "If it weren't for you, I'd be discomfited now." Whom did she think she was talking to? Once, when she said: "When you were little, I often hit you with the cooking spoon," she meant me. And later on, she again meant me when she said: "Your father and you are weavy people. You're always weaving back and forth between home and somewhere else, and you don't find your place either here or there."

When in parting I put some money on the bench for her, she whooped several times for joy, and stomped around the bills in a heavy-footed dance, in which she was joined by some of the other female residents.

I then crossed the square to the church; in the memorial chapel there was a big book containing photographs of the war dead. My father was killed at the very beginning of the war and never saw his son. His picture, which is in a plastic sleeve, does not, like most of the others, show the dark stamplike mustache under the nose, but perhaps he was too young for that when the picture was taken.

From the church terrace, one looks down into the hollow where the Saalach forms the border with Germany— a cold mountain stream with broad gravel banks. One could skip flat stones into the bushes on the opposite bank. Everything in me shrinks back from the country on the far shore—as though that were the beginning of nothingness forever and ever.

That same evening, I stood beside another river. In the early afternoon, I had flown via Zurich to Milan, and from there taken a local train to Mantua. A few kilometers to the south, there is a village named Pietole, which was formerly called Andes and is believed to be Virgil's birthplace. Past the village, behind a dike, flows the Mincio, which Virgil called "immense," making its way "in slow meanders" through the Lombard lowlands, "its banks fringed with swaying reeds." Today, according to certain editions of Virgil, the Mincio is little more than a brook. This, I saw when I got there, is not true; on the contrary, the river answers exactly to Virgil's description of two thousand years ago. In places, it even separates into several arms, with wooded islands in between.

White water lilies with yellow centers rose and fell in the slow current. Little fishes leapt into the air. On one of the wooded islands, a cuckoo called, and a heron glided overhead. Far beyond the river, flames shot into the air from an oil refinery.

It was a warm, bright evening; there was no one about; but a walled-in dog pound gave forth a tumult as of different pieces of music being played backward; and when birds overflew this spot, they would dart vertically upward. I took my clothes off and waded up to my neck into the muddy-brown water.

After dressing again, I went westward into the village and sat down outside a restaurant, the Trattoria Andes. Situated at the intersection of two surfaced country roads, it is surrounded by a large cornfield; almost every one of the half-grown stalks had a sparrow perched on it. This Indian corn was unknown to Virgil, as were the potato plants in the neighboring field, not to mention the tomatoes and the "robinia with its soft little leaves, which rustle more loudly than those of any other tree" (my naturalist son).

On the way back to Mantua, I set off at random across the fields, which are traversed by a number of bridgeless canals. I jumped across most of them; only one was so wide that I had to swim (making a bundle of my clothes and tossing it ahead of me). The weed that we call bear's-breech and feed to rabbits proved, on closer scrutiny, to be something much more choice, the "twining acanthus." The elders here were diminutive. The plane trees, "which lend shade to those who stop to drink," were clipped hedges along the sides of the road; the dried seedpods from the previous year rattled loudly at every gust of wind.

That night, I dreamed that the village of Andes was on a bay along the seacoast. In another dream, I saw my mother's empty bed. Her nightgown was spread out on it; it showed the precise imprint of her bruised body.

Next morning, in Milan, I took a plane to Alghero in Sardinia. It was in Sardinia, in two successive summers, that I begot my children, and once from a passing ship I saw Alghero as a white city. Since then, the city has meant to me "not having to say anything," "the possibility of keeping silent." During the flight, the vacant sea sparkled, and once two ferries passed each other. After the plane landed, there were light-colored baggage checks fluttering on the loaded baggage trucks in the middle of the cement field.

I spent a whole day by the remote Lago di Barratz. Separated from the sea by an enormous dune, it is the only natural freshwater lake on the island. I was alone there. The only sign of other people were footprints. I stood barefoot in the water, over my ankles in black muck, until a tiny leech chewed itself into me, grew fat, and finally fell off. A grasshopper which was almost as big as a sparrow flew onto my hand and I held it between my fingers until its sawtooth legs began to scratch my skin. The shores of the lake were roofed over by tamarisk stalks the color of asparagus, but much taller; their green was in perfect balance with the rippling blue of the water: "the murmuring tamarisk." In the background, on a sand-colored high plateau, a dark bull stood motionless for hours. On the way back to the bus stop, I saw the stone I had killed with lying limestone-gray in the red dust; the round holes in it were my finger marks. I was still walking barefoot, and in the village a child called out to me: "You got no shoes on," and the words became a chorus.

The next day—I should have been back in Salzburg teaching—I passed the home for the so-called retarded in Alghero, which is separated from the sea by a shore road and is called Domus Misericordiae. Nearly all the idiots, young for the most part, were sitting on a long bench in the yard, with their backs to the road; a few sat on the gateposts, looking down at the passersby. One held his fingers to his lips like a Jew's harp and struck them soundlessly. I ventured a look at him. But the idiot on the gatepost won; I lowered my eyes and went away. Toward evening, I went back and again faced the Jew's-harp player, who hadn't stirred from the spot. We took each other's measure at length, impassive but without staring. In the end, there was a blinking behind the fence and my opponent turned away, but with an air of easy indifference, as though nothing had happened, not as one defeated. For the moment, not an idiot, but someone cleverly playing the role. "Ugly fool!" he said.

Next day, on a bus ride to the interior, I tried the

same game with a baby. His face propped on the
shoulder of a woman sitting in the row ahead of me, he
evidently couldn't take his eyes off me; when I looked
back, the baby, as though I had seen through him,
finally showed his profile and took refuge in his mother's
neck; yet at the same time he grinned as though relieved
to be seen through. Mother and child formed a Janus
head. On Sunday morning, on my return to the coast, I
passed the home again; Mass was being said in the open,
under a canopy of trees. Once, a lizard fell out of a tree
and landed on the priest's shoulder. When he raised the
white wafer, it was veined with shadows like a setting
sun. During the sermon, the acolyte played with a spider.
The idiots waved their arms, clapped loudly, and interrupted with inarticulate gurgling, cackling, grunting,
and groaning. A sparrow preening itself in a dusty
hollow turned into every conceivable animal: a mouse,
a crow, a rooster, a lion, a dolphin, a picture puzzle. The
sea off Alghero glittered in far-flung arcs, lines, and
loops, like longhand script. On a block of salt beside it
sat a caged parrot, who didn't say boo.

It was no dream that, some days late, I reported back
to school in Salzburg. My friend in the principal's office
just said: "It doesn't matter," took me to my classroom,
and opened the door for me. On the way, he had given
me a long look, evidently undecided whether to regard
me as a lost soul and failure or as a man changed for
the better.

The building, formerly an imperial cavalry barracks,
is on a bank of the Salzach. The room with its high

walls was very bright. I have never seen eyes of so many different colors, and I thought them all beautiful. The class was strangely quiet, until I said: "Why don't you misbehave? Come on, misbehave a little." My pupils thought I was creepy, and not for the first time, I imagine.

The whitish steam rising from the chimney of the municipal power plant on the opposite bank showed the direction of the wind. By the sounds on the railroad bridge, one could tell what sort of train was crossing: the passenger trains purred and hummed, the freight trains rumbled, and from time to time one heard the clatter of a shunting engine.

I felt happy to be there; to be there not permanently but for the present. I leaned out of the open window, looked upstream, and saw the spray of an arm of the Alm Canal, which drops like a waterfall into the Salzach. For a moment there was a light over the city, which imparted a pastel hue to all the buildings, even the massive walls of the castle. The whole produced the effect not of a backdrop or façade but of a quiet, festive fairyland. Yet it seemed to me that something was gone forever. A part of me had fallen off the cliff with the stoned man. I was no longer among the players, or else I was playing a different game; or, at best, competing for some consolation prize. Melancholy was in the world; it was the reality which deformed and discolored the world. A monstrous picture from Sardinia came into my mind. A colony named Fertilia, built by the dictator's henchmen in the years between the wars: today not a single house has a threshold and the doors to the houses are gaping holes. "Stinking rabble!" I said aloud at my table in the faculty room, which had formerly been the guardroom of the barracks. Someone at the next table retorted: "That will do, Loser." When I looked up, I noticed for the first time that I was one of the older men in the room.

I began my last class of the day by saying: "The Greek word *lalein* corresponds to the German *lallen* (to babble, talk inarticulately). But the poet also calls pebbles *lallai*." I was standing at the window, I saw the spring flow of the river; the wind had drawn a dense pattern of lengthwise stripes extending to both horizons —a regatta of emptiness. I shall be without love, I thought. Shall I be without love? In any case, I shall never again be secure.

Suddenly my melancholy changed to something radically different: to something unprecedented, legendary, unheard-of, and yet instantly convincing. Its name was loneliness and what filled me with enthusiasm was not loneliness considered as my fate but the phenomenon of loneliness. What made the word convincing was an image: outside a house in the early-morning light, I saw the shortest banister in the world, hardly the length of a hand, made for a single step; but it was curved and brightly polished and sparkled in the clear air.

A few days later, I had a powerful little experience in the Oak Tree Colony supermarket. (It is the basis of the present tale.) No doubt as a precaution against shoplifters, a tilted mirror is fitted to the ceiling, and chancing to look up, I saw my face in it. People are always saying that children take after their parents. But what struck me at that moment was the contrary; it is not, as others have sometimes observed, my son who resembles me, but I, the adult, who resemble my son. Ordinarily, resemblances between forebears and descendants strike me as distasteful, if not outrageous; but this resemblance was the opposite; and it would never be noticed by anyone but me. It had to do not with the features but with the eyes, not their shape or color, but their gaze, their expression. Here, I said to myself, I see my innermost being, and for a moment I felt acquitted. In the far corner of the supermarket, in the meat department, two white-clad women were standing in total silence. A car rumbled over the planks of the canal bridge. Outside the display window, there was a great brightness; a vault of light spanned the bridge. But this gaze, I asked myself a little while later—what was it like? And the answer: Wounded.

The following weekend, I went to Gois to see my family. "Gois, Wals, and Siezenheim are good," it is said concerning the three villages on the western fringe of the plain—meaning that they are situated beyond the relatively barren bog. No one was home just then. I went to the toolshed and whetted the scythes, which had rusted during the winter; then I went out to the orchard and mowed the first grass.

The orchard with its many trees and their often interlocking branches is a strange setting for the small "teacher's house," for which flower beds and a lawn would be more suitable. The yellow front is covered by an empty trellis, on which heart-shaped apricots were formerly grown. The whole house seems to have been transplanted from somewhere, from a suburb or residential area of the city, to this remote village. In the bay tree beside the front door—dark green, with translucent veins—linden blossoms, maple spores, and bits of straw from the neighboring fields have come to rest.

It was a rainy afternoon in early May. I chopped wood in the woodshed, hoed the grapevines, which were already putting forth fluffy leaves. Then, at the far end of the garden, I sat down on a grassy knoll which the trees had sheltered from the rain. For a moment, the setting sun appeared.

First my daughter arrived, accompanied by another girl. She had her own key, and the two went into the house without noticing me. Up until then, the stairway had been dark and deserted; now a light went on and legs ran up the stairs. Two heads propped on hands appeared in the open dormer window; pop music rang out, and was softened by the faces of the two listeners; I myself had once had an ear for such music. The girls whispered, giggled, scolded, enjoyed themselves; their foreheads, cheeks, throats, and shoulders had the bloom of demanding yet modest, patient yet self-confident brides awaiting their bridegrooms. O rejuvenated world.

My daughter's mother's car stopped outside the house. She had seen me from the distance and waved. She had treated herself, she informed me, to a little trip across the border, to the Chiemsee, and had taken the boat out to the islands. "Nobody ever comes to see us here in Gois." In the rain, on Frauenchiemsee Island, she had felt so secure that a shudder ran through her. There was a telephone booth in the middle of the lake. A drunk had looked at her "as if he were blind in one eye." In the rainy mist, "the lakeshore had been something like a northern ocean."

As she spoke, I recovered my eye for her. Years before, in the days of our courtship (yes, I was once capable of courting someone!) I wrote to her in a letter: "We come from two different Earths. I from the planet Carefree and you from the planet Care." The present visitor also found a refreshing severity in her face. In confronting most people, I first perceive the Gestalt, the overall picture; in her case, what I see first is the eyes, almost black, and below them the whiteness of her throat. (I know there's no point in trying to describe people, however one goes about it; and yet I sometimes feel I have to say something about her.)

Knowing my son would be on his way home from the athletic field, I decided to head him off. We met on the highway where it passes through a cornfield. Once on the meadow, I saw a clubfooted roadworker with his shovel over his shoulder, walking "under the sky"; that was how I now saw my son, carrying a soccer ball in a string bag, walking under the sky; meandering from side to side of the road, yet determined; and at the same time I heard the scraping of his jean-legs.

The visitor then became the cook. The family gathered for dinner in the winter garden, which is on the west side of the house. My daughter's friend sat down with us; she was to spend the night. The daylight lingered on. Blades of straw glittered in the dung heaps outside the farms; a glow came from the grass under the fruit trees. One could hear the Autobahn—a steady howl. The point where it crosses the border is nearby: a flickering-flaring light as of an oil field between the trees of the semicircular village hill, which with its jagged spruce crowns makes me think of a sleeping boar; the dark hump gives the little white village church on this side of it the dimensions of a cathedral.

It was getting cold on the porch. The guest brought logs and made a fire in the veranda stove. A so-called dwarf palm from the Isle of Silence—a species which allegedly existed only there—waved its fan, and a primitive-looking hare sleeping at its feet twitched a nostril. One of the girls said she wanted a house where there would be a room for everything: a room for stones, a room for plants, a room just for school. A roaring in the east, from the direction of the airfield, meant Frankfurt; another, Linz; another, Amsterdam.

The cook washed the dishes. The woman came into the kitchen with a book, and read aloud a passage from the correspondence of a married couple at the turn of the century: "Your constant absence has given me a higher life, a spiritual drive that would otherwise have remained unknown to me." She added on her own: "One sex says that to another; but mightn't a human being say the same to God?" Then we all watched the television news together, and afterward someone cried out: "But some sort of immortality must be possible!"

I went up to the attic and knocked at my son's door. He said to me in a bass voice: "Don't stand there so respectfully." It seems he had heard from his schoolmates that I had been wandering aimlessly about the town, "like a lunatic"; one had told him how I'd been seen coming out of a public toilet and the attendant had called after me: "Never let me see your face again." He himself had once seen me sitting on a bench between two full plastic bags, "like a tramp."

Only a flashlight was on, and the attic room was in half-darkness. Little knickknacks, mostly metal or glass, gave the wall over the desk the look of a pilot's instrument panel at night. We now had the whole plain outside to ourselves. Green was the last color, then everything turned black, traversed by chains of lights. I sat down on the stool beside my son's desk chair and said: "I have a story to tell you. It's called Threshold Story."

But before the storyteller began, he paused for a moment and said, addressing himself: "Stop. Everything depends on finding the right order." While telling the story, he kept his lids lowered; sometimes his eyes flashed, as though in jubilation. He concluded with the words: "I need you as my witness."

The listener's answer was as follows: "And I thought my father was just a little rebellious off and on."

The narrator opened his eyes, unfolded his hands, uncrossed his legs, sat up straight, breathed deeply, and then looked imploringly over his shoulder into empty space, as though waiting for someone or remembering someone; or as though collecting himself for a very

different story. (A story meant: it was, it is, it will be—
it meant future.) But first he lay down on the floor of
his son's room and slept—someone threw a cover over
him—a night, a day, and yet another night. And he had
a dream: "The storyteller is the threshold. He must
therefore stop and collect himself."

Epilogue

There's a special breeze on the bridge. It's not only the river that creates a breeze of its own; so does the slightly raised canal as it flows across the country. On the surface, the water is so smooth that it seems to stand still, as in a bathtub or a watering trough, while the dark, whirling leaves just below give the impression of a violent current. Both impressions are deceptive; without hurrying, one can keep pace with the birds' nests, paper boats, or chestnut blossoms floating on the surface; if anything, one might have to slow down now and then.

The bridge forms a barely perceptible hump in the plain; still, the moped riders crossing it accelerate, some cyclists stand up to pedal, and the headlights of the cars tilt skyward on the way up. Violet swallows skim the water, in which great bundles of grass drift like uprooted islands. The jagged blackish maple leaves on the bottom look something like bats' wings. The flowing stream seems to be only another form of the stony mountain ridge in the background—its other time form, its dual-aspect picture, its freer manifestation, its lowland self; just as the two frolicking dogs in the meadow to this side of the mountain are only its transposition, its cellular division, its transformation into something infinitesimal but full of life. The two frolicking dogs are transformed into a closely intertwined couple; and the couple in turn into a child with a hood.

On the bank, a lilac bush is in bloom, and toward evening the mountains in the distance take on the color of lilac. An old man is standing on the bridge. His eyes are half closed and he says: "This canal is so quiet, so unassuming, so modest. This water must conquer." A girl in a white coverall stops her bicycle for a moment and, resting one foot on the railing, lights a cigarette. The tall grass at the edge of the road, even the stiff thistles, rustle like reeds in the breeze. A blackbird sings in a willow tree, almost hidden by the foliage but instantly recognizable by its iridescent throat, which changes its hue from note to note. The willow moves when the water beneath it moves. And now a whole country murmurs in the solitary spruce; for a moment, indeed, the sky of all Europe shines blue over the empty bridge.

The first rain dabs circles in the water, which float a little way before losing themselves. The falling snow, however, leaves no trace in the canal; its flakes are instantly expunged by the current. A bright-bellied fish, large for so narrow a stream, leaps high into the air like a dolphin on one side of the bridge, and does it again on the other side. A duck paddles back and forth between the banks like a ferryboat; when a dog comes running, the duck lifts its head and, impassive, lets itself drift downstream. After the rain, steam rises from the bridge and there's a smell of wood in the air.

Whenever a truck drives over the planks, the bridge sways under the feet of the man standing there, as it used to do under peasants' carts; and, at the bottom of the canal, swarms of hitherto invisible little fish scatter. At times, though, there's nothing but water flowing downstream, no objects, no animals—only the pure element; now clear, now cloudy; birch-white, sky-yellow, rock-gray, flesh-colored, cloud-colored, iron-blue, earth-brown, grass-green, peat-black, cistern-black, utterly soundless; only where a branch hangs down into it—or in a narrow place—there's a gurgling as from a hidden spring. Sometimes the element is the color of memory; comparable to nothing, just remembering. Toward evening, glittering spirals drift with the otherwise darkened mass.

In the autumn, they drain the canal and keep it dry for a month; during this time, it is cleaned and the banks are reinforced; the fish are moved elsewhere. The muck stinks. In places, the bed is completely dry, like a wadi. But one fine day the water flows again, muddy, gray, full from top to bottom with odds and ends that have accumulated during the dry period. After exclaiming with surprise that the water is back again, an old woman says: "And how filthy it is!" But adds: "As it should be."

A few of the planks on the bridge have been replaced; for a long while the new planks remain lighter-colored than those around them. Earlier than elsewhere in the vicinity, ice appears in the cracks; later on, it bulges glassy from the clefts in the willow trees. The large, lobed leaf of a plane tree has blown from far off against the trunk of a willow, and there it stays, converted into a special kind of trail marker. One winter's night, seen from the top of one of the "city mountains," the streetlamps along the twisting, turning canal become the most prominent constellation on the plain. Seen from a distance, the meanders twinkle like stars.

The haze that rises continually from the water makes for a distinct zone on either side of the canal; the houses in the Colony, on this side of the veil, become a separate community, with, as its emblem, the old-fashioned wooden wheel which sporadically waters the gardens along the bank. On the far side of the bridge, the pedestrians have arrived, so to speak, on their home ground; up until then, they all goose-stepped on one side of the road, whereas now they band together or scatter as in a kraal or a cattle pen. Immediately after the last plank, a youngster on a bicycle lets go the handlebars and rides home with folded arms. The next rider, whose bicycle lurches and rattles as though on the point of falling apart, alights on the bridge, takes a look at the frame, says aloud to himself: "Oh well, it ought to get me home," and lurches on.

The "bridgeman," also known as the "duty officer" or the "census taker," is inconspicuous; asked what he's doing there, he may answer: "I'm waiting." Waiting, he walks back and forth over the planks, or leans on the railing, propping one heel on the crossbar behind him. He watches as a student driver practices turning at the edge of the bridge. The engine of a parked bus is revving up. The trees of the plain are thinned by the fog. The many black mistletoe balls in their crowns, and beside them, the resplendent full moon. The icy mountain water in the canal cools the heartbeat. At one moment, as he stands here, he is: "I am."

This bridge, he thinks, is so small, there will never be any need to blow it up for strategic reasons. A flag will never be unfurled on it. Under the weight of a tank, it would collapse instantly. Nor is nature likely to show its violent aspect here; in case of flood, the sluice gate on the Ache—where the canal begins—would just have to be closed.

In the Sunday-morning sun, a woman in an advanced state of pregnancy and a young fellow, holding each other by the hand in the middle of the bridge, dance in the presence of the slow current at their feet—dance the pregnancy dance. One night, instead of the usual colored washing in the garden of the lockkeeper's house, where a family of foreigners live, nearly all the washing is white. The viewer finds an unusual word for the activity of the water, the trees, the wind, the bridge: "The canal, the light, the willows, the planks of the bridge—they *prevail*."

A chirping in the wires means that a bus is coming. Ordinarily, one of the alighting passengers hurries ahead of the rest and one lags behind. In the summer, when the passengers jump off the running board in their bright-colored clothes, they look like tumbling ninepins or a riotous band of red-, white-, and brown-skins; in the winter, disguised in their dark clothing and lit by the arc lamps at the turnaround, like refugees or pilgrims. (On this score, we are one with the red Indians.) In batches, they hurry across the little bridge. Not all the homecomers swing their bags like that child now. Rarely does one of the walkers stop and look down at the water (at the most, someone will set his burden down for a moment or shift it to the other hand); a few tap their sticks or umbrellas on the planks. Seldom does one of the bridge crossers curse, grumble, or laugh; but once in a while you hear a narrative note: "When my father . . ." A squeaky shopping cart; a springy baby carriage; a purring electric wheelchair. Then a little stage business: two schoolboys take advantage of the bridge for an exchange they have just agreed upon in the bus, while an adult, after tossing his coin in the box, takes a newspaper out of the plastic bag fastened to the railing. An old woman doubled up with gout stops on the hump of the bridge and squints up at the weather. "Smarty up there does just what he pleases."

The laggard is a young woman; the many different-colored clips in her pinned-up hair glitter and sparkle as she crosses the bridge.

For a moment, the empty bridge is suffused with feminine perfume.

After an interval comes a horse-drawn carriage adorned with garlands and crowded with musicians on their way from one performance to another; they have put their clarinets, trumpets, and cymbals aside and look tired; only the accordion player, who is sitting on the back of the shafts with his instrument in the crook of his arm, opens the bellows on the bridge, producing a long-drawn-out tone.

Now from the medieval canal—as from the medieval figures over the doors of the Old City churches—flow peace, mischief, quietness, gravity, slowness, and patience.